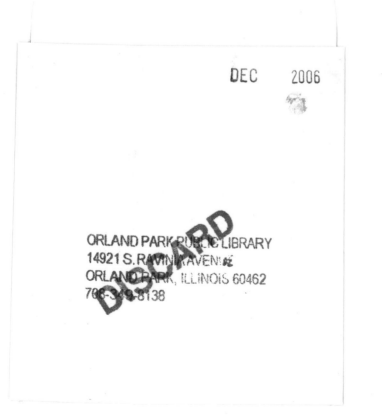

Obsessions
CAN BE
MURDER

A Charlie Parker Mystery

connie shelton

Other books by Connie Shelton

- The Charlie Parker Series
- Deadly Gamble
- Vacations Can Be Murder
- Partnerships Can Kill
- Small Towns Can Be Murder
- Memories Can Be Murder
- Honeymoons Can Be Murder
- Reunions Can Be Murder
- Competition Can Be Murder

Published by Intrigue Press, an imprint of Big Earth Publishing
923 Williamson St.
Madison, WI 53703

This is a work of fiction. Names, characters, places, and incidents either are the product of the author's imagination or are used fictitiously, and any resemblance to actual persons, living or dead, business establishments, events, or locales is entirely coincidental.

Library of Congress Cataloging-in-Publication Data

Shelton, Connie.
Obsessions can be murder / by Connie Shelton.
p. cm.
ISBN 1-890768-75-8

1. Parker, Charlie (Fictitious character)--Fiction. 2. Women private investigators--New Mexico--Fiction. 3. Missing persons--Fiction. 4. New Mexico--Fiction. I. Title.
PS3569.H393637O27 2006
813'.54--dc22

2006026779

Cover design by Brian Schalk, Willems Marketing
Text design and composition by Willems Marketing

Printed in the United States of America

In memory of Wendy.
We all miss you and love you.

My thanks go out to those who read early drafts of the book and commented. Dan Shelton, as always, you know my characters so well and always spot the glaring errors. Susan Slater for suggesting several key points. And to my editor, Alison Janssen, for your pages of thoughtful notes. All of you helped improve the story and I thank you.

chapter

1

FULL SUNLIGHT FILLED the room as I rolled over for the second time this morning and reached for Drake's side of the bed. My hand encountered an empty space and I opened my eyes. The shape of him indented the sheets, but the sound of him came from the bathroom, a happily whistled rendition of "And I Love Her." I smiled and stretched under the covers, warm in the memory of our early-dawn lovemaking.

From the floor somewhere nearby I heard a canine moan as if Rusty were also in some kind of post-coital languor, and the thought made me giggle. As soon as I did, paws scrabbled on the carpeted floor and a red-brown face with perked ears and chocolate eyes appeared at the edge of the bed. This meant just one thing: outside.

I tried closing my eyes and pretending I hadn't seen him, but Rusty's no sucker and when I peeked out through my lashes, he was still sitting there, eyes intent on me.

"Okay, okay," I mumbled, dragging myself from the luxury of the warm bedcovers. I slipped into my jeans and sweater from the previous day and grabbed Drake's jacket from the back of a chair. By the time I'd located Rusty's leash, he was doing a little dance by the room's only door, unaccustomed at home to all these preparations.

We stepped out into a May morning where frost coated the thick grass and blanketed the cars. The Horseshoe Motel was one of those straight out of the 1940s, with individual cabins set in a semi-oval around a park-like common ground. An office building of the same rough-hewn logs guarded the entrance and a sign proclaiming "Jo's Café" stood another fifty yards up the road. Jo's had been closed when we arrived at eight o'clock last night.

Rusty, nose to the ground, dragged me behind him as he circled our one-room cabin and headed for open spaces beyond. Fresh elk tracks were undoubtedly the source of his interest, although I had no doubt that a fair number of rabbits, skunks, and other small creatures had also deposited scent trails for his amusement. Reminding him of deposits, I coaxed him to complete the job he'd come outside for, although I had to admit that simply standing here in the fresh air with sunshine warm on my face and this unbelievably clear mountain air to breathe wasn't a bad way to spend a few minutes.

Watson's Lake, which shared its name with the small town, lay serenely in the still morning air, less than a quarter mile away. On its far side, pine forest rose from the shoreline up a series of hills, ending at timberline a thousand feet or so below the crest of Watson's Peak, where legend says Watson Davis arrived in 1843 and discovered copper, silver, and gold. The discovery had built the fortunes of Watson and of the town.

We'd chosen the location for our four-day weekend getaway on the recommendation of my brother, Ron, who says that the best fishing in the state is to be found at Watson's Lake. Drake intended to test that assertion, while I intended nothing more strenuous than opening a book and occasionally turning the pages.

Rusty eventually circled the cabin and I enticed him back inside with the promise of breakfast, which consisted of a cup of doggie nuggets in his familiar bowl. Drake had finished his shower, as evidenced by the steam floating from the bathroom, and he stood naked at the sink, shaving. I peeled off my clothes and stepped into the shower, surprised to have him join me a minute later. Well, it wasn't a quick shower. When we finally emerged from the cabin we were more than ready for a stack of pancakes at Jo's.

Midmorning sun had quickly melted the frost and the grass now stood dewy and green in the small motel common. We walked up the road, enjoying the view and noticing that half the town must be at the café, judging by the dozen or so cars in the dirt lot near its front door. I looped Rusty's leash around one of the log posts on Jo's front deck and he settled reluctantly to wait.

Drake pulled open a creaking wooden door and flashed me his gorgeous smile as I walked by him. We stepped into the 1950s—chrome tables with Formica tops, chairs of chromed tubing with seats padded in red leatherette. The place went quiet as all eyes turned our way, including those of the middle-aged woman behind the counter—presumably Jo. Drake smiled toward the room at large and raised fingertips to the bill of his ball cap in a tiny salute. A few nods came our way, eating resumed, and the awkward moment passed.

"Sit anyplace you like," said Jo. She wore her frothy red hair up, pinned high with a pink clip shaped like a butterfly. Her voice came out with the deep richness of a smoker, a deepness that would probably turn to a frog-like croak by the time she hit sixty, if she didn't quit the habit soon.

We found an empty table near the long counter, which began near the front door and ran halfway down the length of the room.

"Coffee this morning?" Jo asked, carafe already in hand.

We both held our heavy white mugs toward her. She poured expertly and left us to browse the laminated one-sheet menus that stood at the end of our table, wedged between a ketchup bottle and an all-purpose holder that contained packets of sweeteners and tiny sealed tubs of jelly. I ordered an omelet and whole wheat toast and when Jo had walked away again I noticed that someone had left a newspaper on the seat of the chair beside me.

"Shall we see what the big local news is?" I said, picking it up.

"See if there's a fishing report," Drake said. "Tomorrow morning I'm getting up early again, but with a different purpose in mind."

I wiggled my eyebrows at him because he'd had the same plan this morning, but allowed lust to take over.

"Wow, dramatic photo," I commented, spreading the front page out for him to see. "Fourth Anniversary of Major Fire, Mystery Still Unsolved," I read aloud. The photograph showed a large house completely engulfed in flame. Silhouetted fire fighters aimed hoses at it but the effort, even in print, looked futile.

"Simmons place," Jo said, arriving with our plates. "Burned clear to the ground. Everybody here's pretty sure David Simmons did it himself." She gave me a second to push the paper aside and she set our breakfasts in place. She topped our coffee mugs and turned to do the same for her other customers.

I scanned the article while I made my way through the omelet, which had turned out nice and light, with just the right amount of cheese. The paper described the fire in a way that led me to believe that they'd covered the story in so much depth at the time, this year's rehash was merely to fill space rather than to pass along any new information. The locals had undoubtedly heard the whole thing many times, so the piece was written as a quick recap. Gas leak, arson suspected, house a total loss. A woman, Bettina Davis, had died at the scene, I noted with interest. Davis . . . related in some way to Watson Davis? State fire investigators surmised that she had arrived at the Simmons home and switched on a light, then boom! The paper actually said that—boom. Davis was the housekeeper and it was logical that she would have let herself in with her own key. The home's owners were apparently away, Earleen Simmons in Santa Fe at the time, her husband David last seen driving away the afternoon before the explosion. Insurance investigators called the blaze 'suspicious' and a settlement was pending.

I felt my interest perk up and glanced over at Drake. He'd found his fishing report on another sheet of the paper and was giving that his full attention at the moment. It had been six months since the last case of any interest had come through the door at RJP. Ron, my brother and partner in our small private investigation firm, had secured a lucrative and safe contract doing background checks for a new manufacturing company that moved to the state during the winter. Since they were involved in government work, producing some kind of communications equipment for military bases worldwide, every potential new employee had to pass a screening that was nearly as strict as a top-secret clearance. The money was good but the excitement factor just about nil. I looked again at the picture of the house on fire and felt my pulse quicken.

Stop it, Charlie. Just forget it. This is a long weekend for rest and relaxation. A boat on the lake, a good action novel, late breakfasts, and walks in the forest. I folded the newspaper and pushed it aside. My omelet was delicious and I shoved all other thoughts aside to simply savor it.

"So, you folks staying over for the fishing derby?" Jo made conversation while she filled our mugs once more.

"I saw that in the paper," Drake said. "Next weekend. Guess we'll just miss it." His tone was so wistful that I piped up.

"I could stay," I said. "If you want to. Ron's got things pretty well covered in our office."

"Ought to think about it," Jo said. "There's cash prizes." She picked up our empty plates. "Where y'all from?"

"Albuquerque." Drake said. "I run a helicopter service and Charlie's got a private investigation firm. Much as I'd love to stay and fish, though, it's getting into fire season and I'm on call. Just took this weekend off while my mechanic puts the ship through its annual inspection and gets it ready to go to work."

I noticed that conversations had paused at several of the other tables. Drake has that effect on people. Men, in particular, are always enthralled with his adventures. A guy at the next table turned to him now, and he fell into his routine of answering the customary dozen questions that always crop up. Although I'm also licensed to fly, and have done so on occasion for his business, I have nowhere near the experience necessary to work forest fires. Maneuvering a water bucket on a long-line gets very tricky and takes lots of practice. I limit myself to simple transport—point A to point B kind of stuff.

I watched my husband, in his element now, and realized how much he loved his career. Even on a vacation weekend, he couldn't resist the lure of the exciting adventures he got to perform as routine. After awhile, though, the conversation turned to fishing and he soon had the local men telling him about the best spots on the lake. One of them volunteered his services as guide and offered to take Drake out in his boat near dusk.

Back at the cabin, I pulled out the thriller I'd brought with me and settled into one of the chairs on our miniscule porch, which caught the best of the late morning sun. Rusty flopped near my feet, while Drake began a campaign to clean and organize his pickup truck. While he bunched up bits of trash and doused the instrument panel with spray cleaner, I lost myself in the inner depths of the President's secret underground command center.

"Hon?" Drake's voice snapped me away from a shootout with the FBI. "I'm going down to the little bait shop we saw last night. Get some stuff for this afternoon. I'm supposed to meet Woody at five."

I nodded absently, my pulse on pause until I could get back to the book's action.

"You've been out in the sun for two hours, you know," he said. "Better get inside or find some sunscreen."

I pressed a finger to my forearm. He was right. I sent him off with a kiss and retired to the interior shade of the cabin. Settling into an overstuffed chair in the corner of the small room, I was back in DC until a tentative knock sounded at our door.

Assuming that Drake had forgotten to take a key, I was surprised to open the door to a stranger.

"Are you the private investigator?" The woman was probably in her late twenties or early thirties, with caramel colored hair to her shoulders, the sides pulled back into a clip. She wore a denim skirt and pastel T-shirt with tiny blue flowers on it. Her blue eyes, rimmed by thick, dark lashes were her most outstanding feature. She smiled hesitantly, revealing teeth that had obviously known good orthodonture from an early age.

"How did you know?" I asked.

"It's a small town," she said, letting the smile grow a little wider.

"And I can assume you found our motel room the same way?"

She nodded. "Could I come in? There's something I need to talk to you about."

"Okay."

She must have sensed my hesitation. "Or we could just sit out here on the porch."

By this time Rusty had approached and given her shoes a thorough sniffing. She, in turn, gave him access to her hand and then rubbed his ears briskly. He gave his seal of approval by nudging her hand for more attention.

"Either place is fine," I said.

She stepped forward and I held the door open for her.

"My name is Amanda Zellinger," she said. "And I know your first name is Charlie."

"Parker. Charlie Parker." My, word does spread fast in a small town. She probably also knew what each of us had eaten for breakfast and the license plate number of our truck.

"Jo says you're a private investigator from Albuquerque." At my nod she continued. "I never knew an investigator before, and I wasn't sure where to turn. Now I know. You can help me."

"I'm not sure I . . ."

"It's a missing person case," she said, twirling a strand of her long hair with nimble fingers. "And I can pay you. Uh, if it's not too much. How much would it cost, anyway?"

"We have a daily rate and an hourly one. Hard to say how long it would take. Maybe you can just tell me a little about the missing person. No charge unless we officially accept the case." I indicated that she could take her choice of the overstuffed chair I'd just vacated or the straight-backed one at the small desk in the corner. She opted for the soft one and I sat at the desk.

"My father is the missing person," she said. "It's been four years and no one else, the police or the insurance company, has been able to find him."

"Four years?" Some faint memory niggled at me.

"Yes, it's the same David Simmons who disappeared after the big fire."

So immersed I'd been in my fictional adventure that I'd nearly forgotten the newspaper I'd seen this morning.

"Refresh my memory," I said. "I saw something about this being the fourth anniversary of the fire, but I don't know any details."

"Well, the paper has it right. It was exactly four years ago this week. No one knows for sure what happened. The house simply exploded. Bettina—she was cleaning houses back then and she'd been going to Dad's twice a week—she must have gotten there early that morning. She was killed by the blast. The insurance investigators said it was a gas leak. Probably gas built up in the house all night, they said, then she must have switched on a light or something. By the time the fire department could get there, the whole place was up in flames."

"You didn't live there with your father, I take it?"

"Oh, no. I'm married. My husband, Jake, and I live at the west end of town, up the mountainside where the forest starts to really get thick. Dad married Earleen about five years ago— no, five years before he disappeared." She shook her head. "Sorry, time seems to have stopped since that awful day.

They've been married about nine years now, I guess. Anyway, he built that house for her. The biggest, fanciest house in town. Out there by the lake, it's a beautiful location. I mean, the views alone are worth a fortune. Earleen had a professional decorator from Dallas come up and choose all the furnishings and art. She bragged that Henri—that's the decorator—was going to get *Architectural Digest* out here to photograph the place. It was that nice."

She recrossed her legs and rubbed at her temple. "Anyway, all that's beside the point. I don't care about the house. Earleen has got a new man now, Frank Quinn, and has been on a rant about being unable to collect the insurance money so she can rebuild. And the insurance company has dug in its heels, claiming fraud, saying they're not paying a dime."

"The fact that your father disappeared the same day isn't helping matters, I take it."

Tears welled within the rim of dark lashes. "They think he set it up. They're saying he set the gas on the stove so the house would explode. I know he didn't do it. My father would never have done that." Her voice became urgent. "But it looks bad. He went away that day and he's never come back. If we could just find him and get him to come back, he could explain it all— that it was an accident—and we could all get on with our lives."

My doubt-meter went up a whole bunch of notches. "Amanda, I guess we have to ask ourselves, why didn't he come back? Let's say the insurance people are wrong, the whole thing was an accident—wouldn't he have come back right away to file a claim and try to find out what really did happen?"

"Earleen handled all that," she said. "She did file a claim. That's what she's so furious about now. Dad was going out of town on business. We knew that because he and Jake were working together on a project. Maybe he heard the news about the house and it was too much for him to handle. When it came out that Bettina had died in the fire, maybe he felt so awful that he couldn't face the people in town."

She was grasping at straws, that much was plain, but something inside me felt a strong tug of pity for this girl. She looked so fragile, sitting there in the depths of that big chair, like a small child almost.

"If you can provide me with some basic information about your father—full name, Social Security number, and such—I'll be happy to run some background and find out if he's turned up somewhere else." I quoted her our hourly rate for such work and cautioned her that the police had probably already done the same. She didn't seem to care. She pulled a checkbook from her purse and wrote a check for a five-hundred-dollar retainer.

"I was hoping you'd agree," she said, a night-before-Christmas anticipation brightening her face. "Here. I brought the information with me. And this is the license number of his car." She handed me a sheet of notepaper and pointed out the vitals.

When she left there was a new bounce to her step and I stood on the porch watching her get into a mid-sized white SUV and drive off. Back in the cabin I picked up my cell phone, dialed Ron in Albuquerque, and read off the data to him. The background check would blend so easily into the work he was already doing that it shouldn't disrupt his day. I imagined that he'd have answers for me within twenty-four hours and we'd end up refunding more than half of Amanda's money.

I'd no sooner ended the call than the little instrument buzzed in my hand. Drake, wondering if I'd be interested in a mid-afternoon lunch so he wouldn't be starving during his fishing expedition later. I agreed, he picked me up, and we went to the Burger Shak, a little place we'd noticed earlier. We took a booth along the wall and I noticed only one other couple in the place. They sat at the table nearest the window, their heads together, voices low. Drake likes to sit facing the door so I'd taken the opposite side of the booth and now I spaced out all other thought but the picture of the yummy-looking burgers on the menu.

We ordered—mine with grilled onions and mushrooms, his with green chile and cheese—and Drake talked enthusiastically about the great finds he'd come across at the bait shop. With the fervor of a woman who'd located a shoe sale, he went on about lures and spinners. Men are so cute.

Our food arrived and we were just a few bites into it when I noticed his attention pulled to the front door, behind me. Voices rose as the newcomer greeted the couple by the window.

"I'm going to find him," said a female. "I've got an investigator on the job right now."

With a gulp I realized the voice was Amanda's and she was talking about me.

"And then what?" asked the second female voice. "You're not getting the money, anyway."

The man spoke up. "Yeah, kid. Forget it. Your mom's the one listed on the policy, not you."

I risked a peek around the high edge of the booth. Amanda stood with her back to me. The older woman was half out of her chair. My quick glance registered that she stood a few inches taller than Amanda, wore shiny black leggings and a zebra-striped top, and a cascade of blond curls that fell to her shoulders. She faced Amanda with a look of pure poison. Earleen.

"Dad wanted Jake to have that money for their research. You know he did."

Earleen scoffed. "I know no such thing. That was my home. Your father would never leave me homeless. The money is for rebuilding."

"Well, you're hardly homeless now, Earleen. You've got Frank the sleaze keeping you warm at night."

The slap contacted with Amanda's cheek so quickly I hardly saw Earleen rise from her chair. Amanda retaliated with one of her own, shattering the image I'd had of the helpless little waif who'd sat in our cabin only an hour ago. I spun back to face forward, my eyes wide. Drake half rose from his seat but I put a hand out to restrain him.

"What's going on out here?" The man who'd taken our order emerged from the kitchen.

I heard Amanda whip the door open and stomp out.

"Little bitch," grumbled Earleen, not too quietly.

"Come on." Behind me I could hear Frank's chair scrape back and I turned in time to see him throw some bills on the table and take Earleen's arm. They shook off the insults and managed to leave with a modicum of dignity.

"Whoa. What was that?" Drake asked, reaching for a thick-cut fry.

"That," I said, "was my new client."

⌁2⌁

Drake gathered his fishing gear, stacking everything neatly on the little porch of our cabin. Within minutes, his guide pulled into the driveway and they were off, looking like two school kids on a Saturday. He'd left me with the keys to the truck, a blessing, as I had plans of my own.

Watson's Lake was a town with one main drag, the highway that led, eventually, southbound toward Albuquerque or northbound, very quickly, toward the Colorado border. The section of the highway in the middle of town was called, quite creatively, Main Street. Two or three decent-sized side streets were home to the town's main facilities—elementary school, fire station, town government offices, and a community center. The architectural style was predominantly rustic, lots of rough-hewn cedar, with the occasional stucco for variety. Metal roofs with steep pitches attested to the likelihood of winter snows.

Off those side streets branched a network of meandering dirt roads with picturesque Western names that comprised the residential areas. As one drove deeper into the latter sections, the forest thickened and the roads became more winding. The terrain rose sharply, affording those with more money and, presumably, more prestige to live in large log homes set on impressive outcroppings with windows that gave inspiring views of the lake itself and their humble fellow citizens below. I discovered all this in roughly twenty minutes, by simply driving around.

Actually, my plan was to learn a bit more about the dynamics I'd witnessed an hour earlier, and to see what other clues I might pick up about my client and her missing father. Toward that end, I made my way down the hillside and parked in front of the municipal building, which claimed to house the town clerk, town council chambers, the planning and zoning office, and the county sheriff. A glance at the dashboard clock told me it was a little after five thirty, but three cars sat in the parking area, one of them a sheriff's cruiser. I instructed Rusty to wait in the truck while I went inside.

A cramped lobby featured two straight chairs with orange plastic seats and a dismal-looking rubber plant. The poor thing had enough dust on its leaves to prevent any small ray of sunlight from nourishing it. Behind a glass partition a cubbyhole housed a desk and two file cabinets, probably where a receptionist sat during the day, although the space was dark and quiet now.

"Hello?" I called, hoping some random person would emerge from one of the other three doors that opened into the lobby.

A man in plaid shirt and worn jeans stuck his head out the one with the brass placard that said, LeROY BROWNDOR, MAYOR. "Help you?" he asked.

"I was hoping to catch the sheriff," I said.

"Michaela!" he bellowed. "Got a visitor." He finished pulling a denim jacket on, closed the door of his office, and scooted past me. He offered a weak smile as he pushed open the front door, not one of those huge politician's grins that they give constituents.

"Yes'm." The voice caused me to whip around, and I found myself facing a stocky woman of about sixty. She wore brown denim jeans, a twill shirt in the same shade of brown with a microphone attached to the shoulder, and western boots. A set of handcuffs and a Smith and Wesson .357 hung from her belt. The law enforcement attire seemed at odds with her fluffy white hair, plump rosy face, and first impression of somebody's grandmother.

"I, uh . . . I'm Charlie Parker, RJP Investigations, from Albuquerque."

"Michaela Fritz, Watson County Sheriff. How can I help you?" The set of her mouth and terse words dispelled the grandma image right away.

"We've been hired to look into the disappearance of David Simmons." I felt awkward and stiff and it wasn't working with her. "Look, I'm sure your department has covered this a hundred times. And I really doubt I'll find anything new. But I have this client—"

"Amanda or Earleen?" she asked, the first hint of a twinkle showing in her cool, blue eyes.

"Amanda."

"Not surprised." She shifted to the other foot and hefted the gun belt to take the weight off her back and hips. "Come in my office. It's been a long day."

I followed her through one of the doorways and down a short corridor, into an office slightly bigger than a walk-in closet. Stuffed inside were a large desk and chair, one visitor's chair, and a bank of file cabinets that lined the back wall.

"Welcome to the sheriff's department," she said with a wry curl at the corner of her mouth. She unbuckled her heavy belt and set it on the desk, breathing an audible sigh as she did so. "Ah, well, can't really complain. I'm actually just a deputy out of the county seat in Segundo. Ain't much crime here, anyway, and they can't really justify much in the way of elegance."

"Whatever works, right?" I settled into the visitor's chair as she sank into the high-backed one.

"Well, Roy never did complain about it. Just did his job, right up to that Monday morning when he woke up with chest pains." She shrugged. "I kinda slid into the job, probably because a small-town sheriff tells his wife more about his cases than anybody else. I sorta knew what to do; nobody else did. Election came around, they re-elected me, kept on doing it two more times. So, here I am." She shifted in her seat and discreetly undid the top button of her jeans. "What can I tell you about David Simmons?"

"Anything. Everything. Amanda seems convinced that he went away on his own accord, probably got scared to come back when it turned out that someone died in the explosion."

"Sounds about right," Michaela said. She leaned forward with her elbows on the desk. "Guy drives out of town one afternoon. Next morning his house blows up. He never comes back to find out what happened? Never contacts his wife or daughter? Insurance people were pretty convinced that he set it up to collect on the loss of the house. If that was the case, intentional fire, when somebody dies it becomes murder. Seems like the best explanation why he wouldn't come back."

"Was there physical evidence that might point to anybody else?"

She leaned back in her swivel chair with a deep sigh. Tapped a pencil eraser rhythmically on her desk top. "Arson team comes in, we don't get a lot of the evidence processed through our department. Kitchen stove had the knobs turned to the On position. That tells you something right there. They found a couple of propane tanks with valves open, too, out in the garage. What was left of the garage. Basically, the whole place turned into planks of two-by-four and sheets of metal. Scraps of it flew outward for more than fifty yards."

"Wow. Must have been a mess to sort through it."

"You ain't woofin'. We spent weeks."

"I don't know much about the details of an arson investigation. Were they able to get fingerprints from anything?"

"Some. A few surfaces that weren't exposed directly to the fire, a table here, an appliance or two. They dusted that kitchen stove like crazy. Nothing turned up that couldn't be accounted for within the family. There was a small safe, the kind that's supposed to protect your important papers from fire."

She emphasized the word 'supposed.'

"It hadn't been locked. Explosion probably popped the door open and poof—crispy papers."

"Does any of this evidence still exist?"

"Well, the crime lab folks took everything of value. Eventually, Earleen Simmons had some laborers come out and haul away the sticks of furniture and most of the loose stuff. It took a couple of dump trucks."

"Did anyone—your department or the insurance people— run a check on David's Social Security number? See if he'd gone somewhere else and started working again?"

"Sure. Years ago. I don't know if those insurance people are still following it or not. I think they might have closed the case with a denial of payment. Course a murder case never closes, so that's still out there."

"So David was your prime suspect."

"Yep."

"Any others?"

"One. George "Rocko" Rodman. Bettina's boyfriend. I assume you know who Bettina was?"

"Bettina Davis. The victim. Any relation to the town's founder?"

"Way back, yeah."

"Amanda told me about that. She was David's house-keeper, arrived that morning to clean?"

"That's the story." Michaela fixed a steady gaze on me. "We had witnesses to a fight between David and Rocko the night before all this happened. Down at the Owl Bar. Rocko got to throwing accusations, then he graduated to throwing punches."

"Accusations of what?"

"That David and Bettina were fooling around."

"Were they?"

A shrug. "Who knows. It wasn't the first I'd heard of the rumors, but rumors come cheap in little towns like this. Him married, her with a steady boyfriend—a foul-tempered steady boyfriend. An affair wouldn't have been too smart. But it wouldn't have been the first time for that kind of thing here."

"So, Rocko might have had motive to demolish David's house, maybe take out David in the process." I could suddenly see this getting complicated.

"Or he might have had motive to take out Bettina, and David's house gets it in the process."

More complicated.

"So, what's happened to Rocko in the meantime? He still around town?" I asked.

"Only recently," she said. "He got caught on an auto theft charge, got sent to Santa Fe for three to five. Guess he'd earned enough brownie points to get sprung about a month ago. He's been staying pretty low-key, but he's around."

I pondered all this.

"Trail's gone pretty cold now," she said. "Not enough evidence to bring Rocko back into it, and we'd have to find David to bring him in. We're one of the smallest counties in the state and we just don't have the resources to conduct a national manhunt. If somebody can find him for us, we'll prosecute."

I told her about the background check Ron was doing, but ended up leaving her office without much hope that David Simmons was going to turn up.

The sun hung low in the sky as I drove back to the motel, wondering exactly what evidence the sheriff had against Rocko Rodman. I felt myself being pulled toward the huge number of unanswered questions, the ones that went far beyond my assignment from Amanda—finding David Simmons.

⚔3⚔

The phone was ringing when I walked into our room and I grabbed it up.

"Charlie, is Drake there?" It was Billy, the mechanic who was performing the annual inspection on the helicopter.

I glanced around the room, as if I'd spot Drake in some quiet corner I hadn't noticed before, then realized the foolishness of that. I told Billy he'd probably be back within the hour. I couldn't imagine that fishing could go on much past dark. I'd no sooner hung up the receiver then headlights flashed in the driveway outside. Rusty bounded to the door, vigilant about his new home-away-from-home turf.

Boots stomped on the wooden porch and boisterous guy-talk came through, moments before Drake opened the door holding up a stringer with two nice trout on it.

"Dinner!" he announced.

I gave a skeptical glance around the room, emphasizing the fact that we had no way to cook the things.

"Woody says Jo will cook 'em for us," he said. "Just get your jacket."

We left Rusty with instructions about guarding the cabin and not destroying anything. Jo didn't bat an eye at the request to cook the two trout, just took them, stringer and all, into the kitchen.

Twenty minutes later we had lovely plates of trout amandine before us, and I had to admit it was the best fish I'd ever eaten.

I filled Drake in briefly on my tour of the town and my visit with Sheriff Michaela. "Oh, and Billy called. Just before you walked in the door. Didn't say what it was about."

He got a little preoccupied at that news and we decided to take our slices of apple pie, along with two coffees, back to the cabin so he could find out the bad news. We've learned through experience that maintenance on an aircraft is an expensive proposition, and Drake holds his breath with each inspection that some major component costing tens of thousands won't need replacement. I knew this was the explanation for the firm wrinkle that formed between his brows.

I watched with a little trepidation as he made the call to Billy, relaxed when he did, and started eating my pie when, after jotting some notes, he made another call. From the sound of it he was lining up a job. The bad news was that it would start first thing Monday morning and my little hope of staying over in Watson's Lake for a couple of extra days seemed doomed.

While Drake was in the shower, I called Ron to see what progress, if any, had been made on our search for David Simmons. No answer on his cell or at his house, so I left messages in both places suggesting that he also see what infor-mation he could get from Continental Union, the insurance company in the case.

His afternoon on the lake put Drake into a deep sleep about ten minutes after he'd turned on the television set. I sat up in bed, letting the program's background of intense car-chase music drone on, unable to concentrate on the show. The Bettina-David-Rocko triangle seemed logical, but the Earleen-David-Bettina triangle might be very believable as well. The newspaper article said Earleen was in Santa Fe when the explo-sion happened. When had she left and when had she come home? I should have asked the sheriff more questions. Perhaps Amanda could fill in some of that, too.

I'd already witnessed a not-too-attractive side of Earleen. Maybe I should get to know her a little better. I finally switched off the TV and the lights and lay there in the dark, thinking of the cast in this new drama while Drake snored softly beside me. At some point he rolled over and draped his arm around my waist and I snuggled into him and fell asleep.

I awoke with a vague notion that I might spend the day, Sunday, checking out some of the leads in the case, but Drake had other plans. He was up already and dressed again in his outdoor gear.

"One more day to get in some fishing," he said. "We're going to rent a boat, pack a picnic lunch, and spend the day on the water."

What could I say? Odds were very good that this might be our last weekend together for months. With the fire season kicking into high gear and his aircraft ready to go, he could be away on jobs continuously until August. I layered shirts and light jackets and tucked my book into a day pack. The convenience store at the marina provided sandwiches and chips and sodas. Rusty stood at the edge of the dock with his ears perked, not sure whether he should jump into the boat or not. Ready for a new adventure, though, he joined us.

By noon, we'd caught zero fish, eaten two sandwiches, drunk two sodas, and I'd read only three paragraphs in my book. Not the most auspicious of days. On the plus side, there was still time to pack the truck and get back to Albuquerque, where Drake could go out to the heliport and check over the aircraft, readying the equipment for the next day's job.

The drive went quickly and we got to the house a little after four. While I carried our bags into the house and tossed fishy-smelling clothes into the washer, he began his systematic gathering of equipment from the garage. It's amazing how much stuff has to go along when he leaves for a contract.

After he'd left for the heliport, I sorted through the mail from the past two days, watered my one surviving houseplant, and checked the fridge for supplies although I'm not sure why. Drake would be gone at least a week, probably two, on this job.

There wouldn't be many dinners prepared in this kitchen for awhile.

The phone rang just as I was letting Rusty out the back door.

"Got your messages," said Ron, "just haven't had time to get back to you. You're home now, I guess."

"That's where you called." Sometimes his powers of deductive reasoning astound me.

"Okay, here's the thing. No activity on David Simmons's Social Security number for years. Last reported wages were six years ago from a firm in California—Silicon Valley. Small activity four and five years ago, some self-employment income, apparently, but not much. Since then he's not surfaced anywhere in the United States."

That caught my interest. "Outside the United States?"

"Not sure. There are a few sources I can check, but it gets a lot more difficult."

"Did you get my message about the insurance company?"

"Yeah. They won't tell me much, especially on a weekend. Finding someone with any authority there was impossible. I'll stay on it."

"Any law enforcement activity on David?"

"Not that I could find. Nothing major, anyway. Not to say he might not have gotten a speeding ticket in some little Podunk town, but there's no felony record."

I found myself chewing on my lip. So, where did David go when he drove away that day, and how had he managed to hide himself so well? Most curiously, why had he chosen to have no contact with his family?

Unless he had. Just because Amanda didn't know where he was didn't mean that others had not heard from him. Earleen? I debated the possibility that she and David had cooked up the plan together, but then why didn't she join him wherever he'd gone? Why was she with Frank now if she thought David would come back for her? Too many questions.

I needed to get back to Watson's Lake.

Monday morning began early, with Drake's alarm clock going off at four. We managed a very fast, very hungry quickie before taking short showers and gulping coffee and toast for breakfast. I told him of my plan to keep working on Amanda's case and we both cautioned each other about staying safe on the job.

"I want you to take your pistol with you," he said.

I fidgeted for a second. I hadn't been to the practice range in months.

"Charlie . . . promise me. I don't want you out there completely unable to defend yourself."

"I know, I know." We'd had this discussion too many times.

He pulled me into his arms and held me with nearly rib-cracking firmness. "I love you, baby."

I watched him drive away as a lump formed in my throat.

I packed enough essentials—including the Beretta—to last a few days, waited for the commuter traffic to become unclogged, and gassed up my Jeep to head north. By ten o'clock I passed through Santa Fe and by one I was cruising the familiar-looking streets of Watson's Lake.

At the Horseshoe Motel, Selena Gibbons, the seventy-something lady from Texas who ran the place, greeted me by name. "Didn't realize you'd come back so fast," she said. "I coulda held the room for you." Her blue-white curls stayed firm while her head bobbed.

I thanked her and signed a new credit card slip. I'd no sooner walked back into our same cabin than my cell phone rang. Ron.

"Not much from the insurance company, I'm afraid," he said. He basically recapped what Sheriff Michaela had told me about the suspicious nature of the fire, the fact that David was their chief suspect, and their refusal to pay the claim unless and until his involvement could be disproved.

"Another thought," I said, musing out loud. "Have any of the law enforcement agencies put David's picture out—something like a national alert or APB?"

"I can check, but I don't think so. Aside from the Segundo County sheriff's department, I haven't found other law enforcement agencies who've taken much of an interest. Big things like terrorism and high profile cases seem to draw all their attention. But I'll check."

I walked up to Jo's Café, fastened Rusty's leash to the porch railing, and went inside. The first person I spotted was Amanda.

chapter

4

She was eating alone at a booth near the back, toying with a plate of French fries smothered in green chile and reading a book.

"Hi, Amanda," I said. "May I join you?"

She started at the sound of my voice, but immediately put her book down and indicated the seat across from her.

"Have you found anything new?" she asked.

"Not really. Background, mostly. Stuff you already know, I'm sure." I paused for a minute when Jo approached. Her red hair stood out in a cloud of curls today. I gave her an order for the same thing Amanda was eating. "We're trying to find a contact inside the insurance company who'll be willing to share more of their information, but they seem pretty buttoned up."

At the mention of the insurance, a bright gleam showed in her eyes but it faded when I told her they were still adamant about payment of the claim.

"It just seems so unfair," she said. "They have no proof my father did anything, and he's not asking for the money. Why can't they pay? Jake and I really need—" She busied herself by wiping her hands on her napkin.

"Wouldn't Earleen be the one to collect payment on the house?" I asked. "If they owned it jointly?"

Her shoulders slumped. "I don't know. Jake told me that Dad told him their research work would be funded no matter what. I assumed he meant in case of something . . . something happening to him."

"What's this research project your dad and Jake were working on?" I asked.

"Way over my head," she said with a little grin. "Something medical. Jake's a scientist."

Out here? My skepticism must have came through loud and clear.

"Not everyone in this little town is a hick," she said. "Jake went to Harvard, made some brilliant discoveries in the medical field. They've allowed him to continue his research here—kind of my doing; I grew up in the West and hated the East Coast. Anyway, he has a small lab at home and works on his projects there."

I forked up a French fry and swabbed it in green chile sauce. "And your father—how did he fit in?"

"He always was interested in Jake's research. I loved watching them together, like two little kids with a science fair project. After Dad completed his big merger in California and moved out here, he decided he might help Jake with the financing on the research. You'd have to ask Jake more about that part of it. I have my hands full with a class of fourth graders. While I'm home grading papers at night, Jake is usually out in the lab doing whatever."

"Would he be there now?" I asked. "I'd like to find out a little more. He may remember something David said to him."

"He's probably there," she said. "Whether he'll remember anything new, I don't know about that. We've talked this over so many times."

She looked at her watch and dropped her napkin onto the table. "Oh, gosh, my free period is over in five minutes. I have to dash!" She tossed some money on the table and ran for the door.

I finished my fries, covered the rest of the bill, and walked with Rusty back to the motel where we got into the Jeep and headed down Main Street. I'd snagged the Watson's Lake street map from the motel room and found the Zellinger's address without too much trouble. Take Piedra Vista to Aspen Lane. The biggest hassle was following the winding mountain roads, where number twenty-one might be a half mile from number twenty-three. Once I got used to that part of it, I located the modest wood-frame house on Aspen Lane quickly enough.

The home sat in deep pine forest, with a narrow driveway leading to an attached garage on the right side and a cleared-out parking area directly in front of the house. As with most of the houses I'd seen here, this was done in cedar and redwood, with a steeply pitched red metal roof and wooden deck at the front of the place. Empty window boxes attested to the fact that it was still a bit early for bedding plants here in the mountains, but Amanda had brightened the place with interesting bits of "yard art"—brightly painted wind spirals and two bird feeders, which were being utilized at the moment by a blue jay and four small sparrow-like guys.

I rolled down the Jeep's windows for Rusty and climbed the three steps to the front deck. Large windows gave the occupants wide views of the forest; they also let me see inside quite easily and I could tell that Jake was not in the front part of the house. No television sounds, either.

Beside the front door were two doorbells. A small placard read: Ring this one first. If no answer, ring this one. I followed the small arrow indicating that the leftmost button was to be pressed first. Electronic chimes sounded from within the house, but I wasn't terribly surprised when there came no response. The second button activated an intercom of some sort, apparently, because a male voice came through an overhead speaker, asking who was there.

"Charlie Parker. I'm working with Amanda."

"She's not here. Gets home from school about four."

"I know. I just saw her. Actually, I wanted to talk to you, Jake."

There was a pause. I could envision the scientist at work, disgruntled by this interruption in his day.

"It won't take more than five minutes, I promise."

"Come around back. Follow the pathway to my lab."

I stepped off the deck and discovered that a path did, indeed, lead to the left, where it snaked around the corner of the house. Following it brought me to a separate building, larger than I would have imagined, surrounded by tall pines and connected to the main house by a breezeway. Jake Zellinger was waiting at the door.

He ushered me into a small vestibule, about eight feet by eight. "Leave your shoes, purse, and jacket here," he said. "Don't worry about being barefoot, the floors are heated." He gave me a pair of paper slipper-like things to put on my bare feet.

I noticed that he wore soft slippers with paper booties over them as well. I did as instructed and followed him into a much larger room, probably five or six hundred square feet. A huge desk sat in front of a window with a forest view. Stacks of folders filled most of its surface, attesting to the fact that a clean desktop was low on his priority list. File cabinets stood beside the desk, and the rest of the room was filled with lab tables, including beakers and bottles of liquids. Along the far wall a workbench that looked worthy of any mechanic's shop contained ordinary-looking tools. Ordinary, except that they were all spotlessly clean. I commented on it.

"This isn't the sterile room," he said. "That's beyond the other door. But this one has to stay clean, therefore the 'no shoes' rule."

"Nice facility you have here," I said, looking around. Jake gave a quick tour of the room, pointing out a few charts and experiments of which he was particularly proud. I couldn't follow half of the scientific jargon but gathered that he was an expert in genetics.

"You look awfully young to be this far along in your career," I said, knowing that he held advanced degrees from Harvard, yet he appeared to be barely out of his teens. His dark, longish hair hung unkempt over his forehead, split at the middle by a pronounced cowlick

He gave a crooked, boyish grin. "People say that," he said enigmatically.

I watched him for a moment. I'd placed Amanda in her early thirties. They seemed like an odd pair.

"I'm thirty-seven," he said, finally. "If I look younger than that, it means that our research is working."

My puzzled look spurred him to talk.

"Since the 1980s there's been a small but important research project at Harvard." He picked up a magazine from the desk, a copy of a woman's magazine that looked somewhat out of place amidst the stacks of data-filled sheets. "What are the two things that every person wants nowadays?"

I glanced from the magazine to his face and back.

"To be thinner and younger," he answered. "Look at anything in today's popular press." He waved the magazine then dropped it on the desk. "Every issue carries some newest, latest tip for achieving one or both of those goals."

"That's true," I said.

"We set out to study one of those subjects—how to block caloric intake—and we discovered the secret to both. Actually, the major research is still taking place back East. We've been pursuing molecular pathways that mimic caloric restriction. A couple of years ago a team published a paper on resveratrol, which stimulates this pathway, causing cells to live longer.

"The team has pursued tests on yeasts, then on higher organisms like worms and flies. Long and short of it is that when cells live longer, aging is slowed. Restricted caloric intake means—thinner. Longer living cells means—younger. Ta-da, we have both our goals."

He turned and picked up a folder, reading from a report that contained more four- and five-syllable words than I could hope to absorb. "Basically, we've got the answer but we've needed the means to administer it. Through my research here, I've concluded that an implant of some type was the only practical way. And unlike a lot of medical implants that involve a small device to send electrical energy somewhere in the body, as with a heart pacemaker, this was a different animal. They only way to truly know if it would work was to implant the device in some humans."

I stared at him, the real meaning beginning to dawn. "You've done this procedure to yourself, haven't you?"

"Until I publish my paper next month on the device, which we're calling the YA-30, I can't really say." But the look on his face told me.

"And what was David Simmons's role in all this?" I asked. "He's not a scientist, is he?"

"The other half of every scientific breakthrough is, of course, money," Jake said. "I've been very blessed to have a large institution behind me in the research end of it. But bringing a product to market is an expensive proposition. Patents, proto-types, manufacturing, distribution. There's a lot to it."

"And David had that much money?" I thought of the huge house, the biggest, showiest place in these parts.

"Access. He had access to it." Jake's brown eyes glowed with enthusiasm. "David made a bundle in the Silcon Valley heyday. Had all the right contacts, knew people with fortunes to invest. After I married Amanda he was willing to go along with her wish to live in a quiet rural atmosphere, and he set it up so I could have this lab and continue the important research work.

"He had the marketing brains, developed a plan to hook up with his venture capitalist friends, bring the product to market on a five-year time frame." Jake dropped the folder on the desk. "That was four years ago."

"What did David say to you, right before he left?" I asked.

"Pretty much what I just told you. He had a meeting with some guys in Denver. I was under the impression he'd be coming back with a big check—over a half million—with more to follow." He shrugged. "We never saw him again."

I thanked him for showing me around and promised not to breathe a word about his invention—not that I would know how to effectively leak a big, scientific story anyway. Back in my Jeep, I picked up the phone directory for Watson's Lake and looked up Earleen Simmons's number. But when I tried using my cell phone I got a No Service signal. Too close to the mountainside, I decided. I'd try again when I got down to the highway.

I found myself wondering, as I drove the meandering dirt roads, about the dynamics of the list of suspects I'd begun to build. Who, other than David, had reason to set fire to the house?

⚛5⚛

Rather than phoning ahead with a warning, I looked up Earleen's address, which was listed under Frank Quinn's name, and with my little trusty map found my way to an A-frame house two blocks east of the elementary school on one of the town's narrow side streets. An elm tree in the front yard was making a valiant attempt to leaf out and some hardy mountain grass, thick with blooming dandelions, gave a layer of color to the otherwise drab surroundings. The house itself hadn't been painted in years and leaves from the previous autumn had gathered in sodden clumps at the corners of the raised porch. Not finding a doorbell, I rapped at the cheap wooden door.

Voices from a television set blared, followed by chirpy music, and I knocked harder the second time. The sound instantly went mute and a few seconds later the doorknob rattled. Earleen opened the door and stood squarely in the opening, facing me with the same degree of friendliness she probably reserved for insurance salesmen and Jehovah's Witnesses. Her blond hair was piled on top of her head in a froth of curls and the smoke from her cigarette caused her to squint through her right eye.

"I'm Charlie Parker, RJP Investigations. Could we talk for a minute?" Although she flashed me a look of curt impatience, she stepped aside and I followed her Lycra-clad behind into the living room.

"You the dick Amanda hired?" she asked, surveying me cynically.

"I haven't heard that term outside old movies, but I guess the rest of the statement is correct."

"Who was that?" a male voice shouted from another room. "Nobody, Frank," she hollered back.

Well, that stung. She plopped herself onto a flowered sofa and set the cigarette on the edge of an ashtray, picking up a glass of golden liquid. "Something to drink?" she asked.

I declined and took a chair that I could tell immediately was going to force me to either perch primly on the edge or sprawl back helplessly into its well-sprung cushions. I opted for the prim perch. A glance around the room told me that Earleen had taken a big cut in lifestyle when David left. From everyone else's descriptions of the huge house by the lake, it had been quite elegantly furnished by a professional decorator. If a decorator had done this place, he or she had come from the thrift shop school of design.

She took a long drag on the cigarette and blew a long, showy plume of smoke toward the ceiling.

"Think you're going to convince the insurance company to give Amanda the money?"

Wait a minute, I'm supposed to ask the questions. "She just wants me to find David. I'm trying to retrace his steps and find out where he went."

"Yeah, well, good luck. I know he planned to drive up to Denver. I went to Santa Fe that day, shopping. Ended up staying over, had a nice dinner and a couple of drinks. It seemed better not to get out on the road." She paused to stub out the cigarette. "Got home the next morning to find out that my home was gone, my husband disappeared. I was a wreck. They had to carry me away and give me sleeping pills. Have you ever had to stand and look at the burned out wreckage of your home?"

Actually, I had. But I put myself back in the role of questioner, not questionee. "So, you have no idea whether David went or what time he left?"

"Like I said, he planned to drive to Denver. When the sheriff asked all these same questions, somebody told her that they'd seen him driving away around five o'clock. That's all I know." She lit another cigarette from a pack on the end table.

"Four years have gone by," she continued. "I've gotten on with my life. Don't get me wrong. I loved David. God, that man was my dream come true. But a woman's got needs, you know? My dream man is gone, my dream house is gone. I just want them to hurry and settle this thing so I can rebuild and go forward."

The answer to Earleen's needs walked through the room just then and I got a better look at the man she'd been eating with at Jo's a couple of days ago. Frank Quinn wore a dingy pair of Levi's and a tank style undershirt which hung loosely on his thin frame. Dark blue tattoos covered both arms and his shoulder-length hair looked as if it hadn't been washed in a week. He shot an unfriendly stare toward me but continued toward the kitchen without a word. Rounding the counter that separated the two rooms, he pulled a beer from the refrigerator, popped the top on the can, and took a long drink. With a belch he retraced his steps and disappeared again.

Earleen must have read my thoughts. "Hey, Frank's a good man," she said lowly, leaning forward. "He's just been tied up with a big project all morning and didn't take the time to dress up."

"I can see that."

"Don't you be judging me or my situation," she said. "I've had more tough times than you can even imagine. David's leaving me just broke my heart. If only he'd come back to me . . ."

She even worked up a tear for that last part.

"Look, I'm not judging. It must have been rough. I can't even imagine." And, truthfully, I couldn't.

"Alls I want now," she said, "is to get this thing settled. If David's not coming back I should get the money for the house. If, heaven forbid, something's happened to him, then there's some life insurance too. I just want what's coming to me."

The words sounded about right, but the tone told me that she no more wanted David to come walking back into her life than a Popsicle wants a warm oven.

"So, what does the insurance company say about all this?"

"Nothing for the house unless somebody can prove David

didn't cause the explosion. How'm I supposed to prove that? I wasn't even here." She worked agitatedly at the ash on the cigarette. "They won't declare him dead for seven years. I had ten thousand in a joint checking account, and let me tell you, that doesn't go very far towards paying the bills for four years. So, I've basically got nothing." This time the tear was genuine.

"It's a bad situation," I acknowledged. "So, you don't mind if I keep asking around, see what I can find out?"

She gave a little wave that indicated assent and I pried myself up from the sagging chair.

"One other thing," I said as I walked toward the front door. "I heard there was rumor of something going on between David and the housekeeper, Bettina Davis? Did you know anything about that?"

Her face hardened and all trace of the vulnerable tears vanished instantly. Her shoulders went back, her sizeable breasts upward. "I was plenty of woman for my husband," she said in a voice of steel. "He had no reason to go looking anyplace else."

I nodded and walked out. Her answer told me more than she probably intended.

It was a little early for dinner but my stomach was speaking to me so I decided to drop in at Jo's for a piece of pie or something. Rusty happily waited in his familiar spot on the porch while I went inside.

The small diner was empty and Jo sat at one of the counter stools, indulging in a private moment and a cup of coffee. I felt guilty asking her to get up.

"No problem," she said. "Lemon meringue's good today. Want some?"

She cut a generous slice of the pie and brought coffee to go with it.

"So, you're the investigator Amanda Zellinger's hired, huh." It wasn't really a question.

"This really is a small town." I laughed as I slipped my fork through the cool lemon filling.

"Not much I don't hear about, sooner or later." She picked up her own mug again and stood across the counter from me while I ate.

"Yum, this is really good," I said after the first bite of the pie. "So, I hear the rumor is that David Simmons and Bettina Davis might have been having a little fling?"

"That one almost stayed secret," she said with a twinkle in her eye. "David was pretty discreet. Bettina, now—" She rolled her eyes. "She'd targeted just about every halfway decent guy in town at some time or other."

"Really?"

"Poor girl. I gotta be fair. She just wasn't real bright. One of those girls in high school who wasn't popular 'cause she wasn't pretty, didn't have money or nothing. Somewhere around her junior year she started putting out for the guys. Well, you know how long it took for the reputation to spread. In this town? About five minutes. Guess both she and the guys had a pretty good time of it for a couple of years. But they all graduated, moved on. Times have changed—a lot. But not that much. No guy, to this day, wants to marry the girl who's screwed every one of his friends. Poor Bettina found out that her popularity was based on one thing only and it really came back to haunt her."

"Hm, too bad."

"Yeah, it really was. She was a sweet girl. Could have turned out a whole different way."

"But she did have a boyfriend near the end, didn't she? What was his name?"

"Oh, you mean Rocko Rodman? Ugh. Slime. I felt bad for her, dating this loser, rap sheet that went back to vandalism when he was about eight or so. He'd latched onto her because, in an average way, she was kind of attractive. Would have been more so if she'd left off half the goppy makeup, but that's the way it was. Rocko has this sort of dangerous attraction for women, you know? The bad-boy biker, the rebel-without-a-cause type."

She paused for a minute and topped off both our coffee mugs. I pressed the tines of my fork against the last of the piecrust crumbs and licked them off.

"They'd only been dating for a few months, I think. Long enough that he thought of her as 'his woman' and short enough that she hadn't gotten sick of it and broken it off yet."

"There was an argument between him and David, wasn't there?"

"Guess so. I didn't see it, but heard they actually threw a few punches over at the Owl—the bar."

"Any chance Rocko took it further than that? Set up the explosion, maybe?"

She glanced at the door and I turned to see that a couple with two little kids were getting out of a car outside. Jo leaned in closer to me and lowered her voice. "I wouldn't be at all surprised. I've thought that from day one."

"Did the sheriff ever follow that line of questioning?"

"Michaela? No way. She didn't want to hear anything negative about Bettina."

My brows pulled together.

"Hello?—family. Bettina was her niece."

chapter

<del>&</del>**6**<del>&</del>

I left money on the counter and thanked Jo as she turned to wait
on her new customers. Outside, Rusty greeted me with that
enthusiasm that dogs always seem to work up, no matter how
long or short a time you've been apart. I patted him briskly and
led him to the Jeep, all the while wondering about the complex
web of relationships that had managed to form in this little place.

Had David been the intended victim, after all? Or had
Rocko gone back to his roots in vandalism to simply destroy his
enemy's most prized possession? Perhaps more sinister—
because of the amount of planning involved—had Rocko rigged
the house to explode, knowing that Bettina would be the first
one to walk in the door the next morning?

Somehow, I couldn't see a guy whose criminal career consisted of spraying graffiti, stealing cars, and starting bar fights
having the smarts or the reasoning power behind that latter sce-
nario. He'd have had to know that David was leaving town,
when he would leave, how to get into the house, past any alarm
systems, and also the fact that Earleen was going to be away
overnight—it all seemed a tad sophisticated for his level of crim-
inality. On the other hand, I'd already seen firsthand how easily
information passed around this tiny burg. It wouldn't take a
rocket scientist to know how to set up the Simmons household
for a hit.

I drove to the motel and parked, giving Rusty a chance to
run out behind the buildings while I tried to figure out where
to go next with my questions. I had a hard time envisioning

someone of David's caliber, a man from a bigger city, a more sophisticated environment, wanting to take up with a girl who'd never kept her legs crossed. But stranger things had happened and I decided I needed to know more about the victim.

I called Rusty back and coaxed him into the car once more.

Sheriff Michaela sat at her desk once again when I walked into the town offices. Again, no receptionist in sight at the front desk, so I entered on my own.

"You're back, huh," said Michaela, looking up briefly from some reports she was signing.

"Yeah, it looks that way. The family still wants answers."

She shot me a quick look. "They know just about all that we know," she said.

"I don't think it's that, so much. Amanda just has this hope that her father will come back someday. She's clinging to the hope that I can make that happen."

"Well, good luck." She signed one last form and closed a folder over the pages as I took the seat opposite her desk. "So, what can I do you for?"

"Bettina. I wonder if you have a photo of her."

"Don't see where that's going to lead you to David Simmons," she said stiffly.

"Not directly, no." I felt my way carefully along the slippery slope of family ties. "She was the victim in this crime. Her, uh, boyfriend got into a fight with David. I guess I'm just curious about her. Wanting to put a face with the name, wanting to get some kind of sense of knowing her as a person, not just a name on a form. I know she was your niece. This must have been very painful."

Michaela softened a little. "Crime scene photos aren't going to tell you much, and, frankly, I can't stand to look at 'em myself. Hold on a minute."

She unlocked one of the file cabinets and pulled the bottom drawer open. From it she withdrew a surprisingly feminine purse made of quilted fabric in shades of pink and blue. The contrast with her brown uniform with its badge and weapon was striking. From the purse she pulled a light tan wallet and withdrew a plastic holder for photos. Flipping through them, she came to one and pulled it out.

"This was taken her senior year of high school. About four years before she died." She looked at the photo fondly before handing it to me. "She looks so young here."

I took the picture and studied it. The girl looked very average. Nice eyes, dark brown with thick lashes, a full mouth with the hint of an overbite that might tend to make her look gawky in reality although that didn't come through strongly in the photo. Mousy brown hair framed her face in curls that looked as if they would be difficult to tame. I could see where Jo's appraisal might be accurate—the insecure girl who never quite made it into the popular crowd. The vulnerability came through and I could also see where males would be attracted, either as protectors or as predators. There are both kinds out there.

"Thanks," I told Michaela, handing the photo back to her. "She was very sweet looking."

"She was. Sweet." She shook her head slowly. "I know about her reputation with the boys. I tried to talk to her about it. That was difficult. She was so insecure and any little thing that came across as criticism . . ."

I nodded.

"I made sure she was on birth control. Which was more than her mother, my sister-in-law, would do. That woman lived in denial almost every minute of her life. Poor Bettina." She stared at a spot in space.

Yes, poor Bettina. Everyone seemed to refer to her that way.

"The more questions I ask, the more questions crop up," I said, finally. "Everyone connected with David seems to be a possible suspect."

She busied herself putting away her wallet and purse.

"Could we run over the alibis that everyone gave at the time?" I asked.

Michaela shrugged. "Don't recall that anybody but David really had to provide one. Course, he couldn't."

I guess impatience flashed across my face because she shifted slightly in her chair, then got up. Pulling open one of the file drawers behind her, she reached in and took out a thick folder. She flopped it onto the desktop.

"Okay. Let's review the statements we took." She opened the folder and set aside a nine-by-twelve manila envelope. "Crime scene photos," she said. A stack of newspaper pages followed, and she set them aside as well.

The pages of reports and interviews were fastened into the folder with a silver prong and bar clip at the top. I watched powerlessly as she slowly scanned the pages and flipped them, beginning at the back of the file.

"Got the initial call at 7:14 a.m. Fire department responded at 7:36, found the entire structure engulfed in flames."

She heard my small hmmm.

"It's a volunteer fire department. And the house was on the far side of the lake."

"I didn't say anything."

"Arson investigation team from the county seat arrived at 10:07. Began a preliminary on the scene, although it was still pretty hot at that time. The woman of the house, Earleen Simmons, arrived at 10:31, immediately became hysterical, had to be forcefully removed to an ambulance where paramedics calmed her. I took her statement. She said she'd been in Santa Fe the previous day and overnight."

"Any proof of that?" I interrupted.

She shot me a look. "Didn't ask for it. The woman was clearly distraught." She turned back to the page. "I asked who else might be in the house and she didn't think anyone was. Her husband had left for Denver the day before, she said."

"Was she the witness who said she saw him driving away?"

Michaela scanned the page quickly. "No, there was somebody else . . . I'll come to it in a minute. As I was talking with

Earleen, I remember that's when someone shouted that they'd found a body. At that point Earleen fainted and I left her with the paramedics.

"The body was burned beyond recognition so we had the medical examiner's office come for it." She looked up from the file and took a deep, steadying breath. "Later, it was identified as Bettina and when I questioned her, Earleen remembered that it had been their scheduled cleaning day."

"And the witness to David's driving away?"

She shuffled a few more pages. "Guess I didn't write it down. It wasn't really a formal statement, but Jake Zellinger was one of them, I remember. Late afternoon of May 11th, he and Amanda were driving down to Red River, going out to dinner for her birthday, as I recall. David's car was a red Mustang convertible. Pretty easy to recognize, even at a distance, around here. Most everyone drives pickup trucks or SUVs. Somebody else—can't remember who it was—mentioned seeing the red car driving north out of town. You know how people talk about a tragedy like this for weeks afterward.

"Once the arson folks decided the gas leak wasn't accidental, the talk really notched up. You know, people always remember where they were, what they were doing, when something bad happens. That's when it came out that David had this big argument with Rocko Rodman the previous day."

"And you thought maybe Rocko set it up so David would be killed in his own house?"

"Seemed logical. Hot tempered—always. He shouted a lot, and then he tended to bust up things. Break windows, vandalize a car, that kind of thing. It made sense that he and David get into this big screaming match, then he goes off and lets the steam build up, decides later to torch off David's house."

"Matches and gasoline weren't good enough for him?"

She shrugged. "Who knows what goes through the mind of a guy like that. He's a druggie and pretty much a nut job."

"You interviewed him formally, I guess?"

"Of course." She stiffened at my question, although I truly hadn't meant anything by it. She turned to a new page. "According to his statement, George "Rocko" Rodman was at home the afternoon and evening of May 11th, sleeping off a hangover from the previous night and early morning. That would have been the night he got so drunk and confronted David—May 10. No one could verify this, but his motorcycle was in the driveway of the apartments where he lived."

"Was he ever arrested?"

"Lots of times, but not for this. Never did find any physical evidence that tied him to the scene. Not much you can do these days unless you can build a strong court case. Couple weeks after the fire, Rocko got caught on an auto theft and that one had plenty of evidence. Sent him down to Santa Fe and hoped to be rid of him for good. Guess not, though. He did his time and, like a bad penny, has shown up here again."

I got the address where he was apparently living with a brother, who rented a house on Quarter Horse Road. Maybe I'd drop by and ask a few questions, but I wasn't sure what I could hope to learn. Outside of a bout of remorse and a full confession, there still wasn't enough to tie Rocko to the crime.

"Anything else you can think of?" I asked Michaela. "Anything I could report to Amanda concerning her father's whereabouts?"

"Nothing she doesn't already know," she said, shaking her head. "I do know that Earleen's pushing to have David declared legally dead. Guess she thinks she can do some kind of legal maneuvering to get around the statute requiring seven years. Got a strong thing going with Frank Quinn, you know."

"So, wouldn't it be more logical to just file for divorce against David? Quicker?"

"Quicker, yeah. But then she wouldn't be in line to get

anything from the insurance. It would probably automatically go to Amanda as his next of kin."

I thought of Earleen's bitterness over her current living conditions, how adamant she'd been about her right to get back into a big, fancy home and have some money to spend. How angry was she?

⋑7⋐

I spent a restless night, alternating between my usual low-grade worry about Drake anytime he was out flying forest fire contracts and the myriad information about the case that kept floating persistently through my head. By five o'clock I was completely awake, staring at the pale light in the room.

Amanda would be leaving pretty early for school, but maybe I could catch her. Five just didn't seem like an appropriate hour to call anyone though. I dressed warmly and took Rusty out for a walk across the frosty grass. He seemed overjoyed at the chance to explore all the strange animal smells at his leisure. Across the open field behind the motel, I spotted a herd of elk, unconcerned, simply munching on the grass. I reined in the dog and froze in place to watch them until some small noise startled them and they bolted, as a group, running effortlessly on their strong legs toward the tree line. I counted twenty-three of them.

Rusty watched them, his ears perked in curiosity, and when they'd all disappeared into the forest he turned to look up at me. Both our eyes were wide with wonder.

We finally broke our trance to head for Jo's. By now it was six o'clock and she'd just flipped over the Open sign. I went in and came out a minute later with a bag containing two donuts so fresh they were still warm and a Styrofoam cup of her fragrant coffee. Back at the room, I figured the decent hour had arrived and I dialed Amanda's home phone as I bit into the first of the donuts.

"I hope it's not too early," I said.

"I'm not going to work today," she told me and I caught a distinct tremor in her voice. "Someone ran me off the road last night. My car's totaled."

"What!"

"Not far from the house. Just as I made the turn off the highway onto Piedra Vista."

"Are you okay?"

I heard her take a deep breath. "Physically? Yeah, I think so. Sore muscles are showing up this morning in places I didn't know I had muscles."

"Do you know who did it?"

"It was so dark. I couldn't tell much about the other vehicle. They didn't stick around."

"I'll come over."

"Jake's here. I'll be okay."

"That wasn't quite what I meant. I'm wondering if this could be connected to the case."

A long silence came over the line, as palpable as a hum. Finally, she said, "Yes, maybe you better come."

I wolfed down the rest of the donut and took the other one, the coffee, and my purse with me. I missed one turn as I tried to remember the way to their home, but still managed to get there within ten minutes.

Jake opened the door and greeted me with a solemn face. "She's in here." He led me through the small foyer into a den whose most prominent feature was a big-screen TV.

Amanda lay on a leather sofa, propped in one corner with several large pillows and bundled into a fuzzy blanket of some sort. She held a mug of hot chocolate between her palms, pulling the warmth from the ceramic.

"I'll leave you two to talk," Jake said.

"He's got to be glad you came over," she told me after he'd closed the back door. "I could tell he was itching to get out to his lab but felt obligated to sit here with me."

Her face bore the ravages of the accident—both eyes were deeply blackened, and a small row of stitches tracked over her left eyebrow. Her hair hung in greasy strands and a smear of blood hadn't yet been washed from her chin.

"Guess I won't be going back to work until I can do so without scaring the kids half to death," she said with an attempt at a smile. I noticed that one of her front teeth was chipped.

"What happened?" I asked, kneeling at the side of the sofa.

"I'd stayed late. We're doing parent conferences this week, and I'd scheduled a couple of them for the evening, for people who can't come earlier. It was probably eight or so when I got away. Dark already. Nothing seemed out of the ordinary. I just headed home." Her voice wavered and she took a deep breath. "I'd turned off the highway and all of a sudden there were headlights right behind me. I swear, one minute there's nothing back there and the next minute, the lights are right on me. The car—actually I think maybe it was a pickup truck, the lights were pretty high off the ground—well, it kept coming closer and closer. I sped up a little, but the road is so winding, I couldn't go much faster. I was so scared."

Her hands had begun to tremble and I took the mug of chocolate from her and placed it on the coffee table.

"I decided I'd just pull over and let him pass, but when I got to the side of the road he bumped me. I lost control and went off into the drainage ditch. With the speed and all, I couldn't hold it. My car rolled. I just remember the air bag hitting me in the face. Then I was upside down, hanging by my seatbelt." Tears spilled from both eyes. "The worst part was when I tried to move. My weight shifted the whole thing and it rolled again. I ended up hanging sideways, screaming, wondering if it was going to just keep rolling forever."

I reached out to hug her but she flinched in pain.

"Everything hurts," she said. She pulled back the shoulder of her sweatshirt to reveal a nasty purple stripe on her left shoulder where the seatbelt had saved her life by scraping and bruising a swath of her skin.

"Jake found me," she whimpered. "Luckily, I'd called him as I was leaving school. When I didn't show up, he came looking. He was pretty shaken, especially when the sheriff ordered an ambulance to get me. We were in Segundo almost all night."

"I'd like to ask you a few questions, if I could, then I'll leave you to sleep."

She nodded and reached toward the mug of chocolate. I handed it to her.

"You said you didn't recognize the other vehicle. Think really hard. Can you narrow it down to what kind it was or what color?"

"Big, like I said. Probably a pickup truck or a big SUV, like a Suburban or something. Dark, I think. But the lights were so bright in my eyes."

"Can you think of anybody who owns a vehicle like that?"

"Just about everybody," she said. "This is a mountain town. If you don't have four-wheel drive and high clearance, you don't make it through the winters here."

"Do you think the other vehicle sustained any damage? Think. What part of his car hit yours?"

She squinted in thought. "I guess it would be his right front section. But he didn't actually hit hard. Just came in close and nudged me off. If only I'd steered in the other direction, maybe. I don't know."

The tears threatened to spill again and I waited quietly while she composed herself.

"I'm sure Sheriff Michaela asked you all this stuff already. I'm sorry to put you through it again."

"It's okay. I'd rather you did it. I don't think Michaela is especially understanding toward me."

"What do you mean?"

"Oh, it's probably nothing. She's just been chilly lately. One of her grandkids is in my class and I just get this feeling whenever she comes around. It's been that way since the other . . . the fire and all. She didn't like my dad and she's not crazy about me either, I guess."

I wondered where that came from. I hadn't sensed any ill feelings when I talked to Michaela, but then I'd never seen her interact directly with Amanda either.

"Are you saying that you don't think she would thoroughly investigate a crime—either this one or the fire—just because it involved your family?"

Amanda shrugged but it turned to a wince of pain.

"Okay, I'll poke around, see what I can find. If, like you say, she's not doing a thorough investigation, we may turn up some additional evidence." I asked her if there was anything else I could do for her and she had me retrieve a small wireless intercom device from the kitchen counter so she could call Jake out in his lab if she needed anything.

"I'll be okay," she said. "Sleep and painkillers will get me on the road to recovery."

I locked the front door behind me and went back to my Jeep. Rusty waited patiently, fogging up the windows with his doggy breath. As I drove away from the Zellinger house I wondered what was going on here. Would Michaela actually subvert a police investigation because she didn't like the victim? I thought about the fire and the fact that Bettina was Michaela's cousin, the poor girl everyone felt sorry for. Maybe Michaela had a personal interest in seeing David Simmons pay for the crime, and maybe she'd never seriously pursued any other possibilities.

But how did that relate to Amanda's close call? Someone had tried to kill her and I felt a steely resolve to find out who and why.

chapter

⇥8⇤

I spent the next hour and a half cruising the town, including a lot of winding residential roads, looking for a large vehicle with a broken headlight or damage to its front fender. As Amanda had warned, about half the vehicles in town fit the description in size and color. And by including the lighter colored ones, I discovered her assertion was true—it could be just about any one of them. And the bad news was that I didn't spot one with the kind of damage she'd described. Either the vehicle hadn't sustained so much as a broken headlight, or someone had wisely parked it in a garage.

At Woody's Chevron—the same Woody who'd been Drake's fishing guide—I found Amanda's mangled Blazer, still resting crookedly on the bed of the tow truck. I pulled over to take a look, just as Woody himself came walking out.

"Hey," he said in a friendly tone. His mouth barely revealed a set of even, white teeth between the overhang of his dark mustache and the abundant growth of beard below it.

"Hey," I said back. "This is Amanda Zellinger's vehicle, isn't it?"

He nodded solemnly, giving me a sideways look.

"I'm Charlie Parker," I said. "You took my husband Drake fishing a few days ago."

"Oh yeah. Helicopter pilot. You're the investigator."

"I was just over at Amanda's. She's pretty bruised up."

"She okay though? Sweet gal. Looked pretty shaken when they put her in that ambulance last night."

"She'll be okay, I'm sure. In a few days." I'd worked my way around to the rear end of the Blazer's crumpled remains, looking for any trace of contrasting paint against Amanda's own white. "Any idea who might have done this?"

He unlocked the truck and started to climb inside. "Sheriff was there. You might ask her." He started the tow truck and drove it through an open gate behind the station, into a chain-link enclosure. I trotted along beside and waited until he'd killed the engine and climbed back out.

"I'll talk to Michaela, for sure. Just wondered whether you'd heard anything. It's a small town."

He shrugged and turned to work a set of levers on the side of the truck. A hydraulic motor whined and the bed of the truck began to tilt the load aft. I stepped back and watched in fascination until the Blazer rested on the ground and the truck was ready to drive away.

"Guess there'll be an insurance adjuster coming out to decide that it's totaled," I said. I circled to the back of Amanda's vehicle again and studied the rear bumper. Near her broken-out taillight, just below the side window, was a small smear of red paint, in clear contrast with her own white.

"Yep."

"Woody, you're a man of few words, I can tell, but give me a break here. You're a professional when it comes to cars and damage. You've got to see all kinds of wrecks. Can you give me any little clue about who might have caused this?"

He paused with one leg already in the cab of his truck. "I'm a family man, don't hang out at the bar much, but I'd look there, I was you. Somebody had a few too many last night."

I considered that as he started the tow truck once more and drove it around to the other side of the building. Could it be that simple? A drunk driver? In Amanda's mind the collision was no accident and someone had deliberately come after her, but the terrifying moments of the crash may have magnified it all in her mind.

I walked back to my Jeep, thinking it all over.

Outside Jo's Diner the breakfast crowd was out in force. I pulled into the lot and parked next to the brown and gold police cruiser, an Explorer four-by-four I'd seen at Michaela's office on my previous visits. As I walked toward the door I checked out the front fenders of every red vehicle in the lot but I wasn't destined to get that lucky.

Every table in Jo's was occupied, primarily by men in denim and plaid, working guys getting a big breakfast before heading out for the day. Jo nodded from across the room as she circulated among the tables with her coffee pots in hand. I spotted Michaela alone at a table and I pulled out the chair across from her.

"May I?"

She nodded and pushed her morning newspaper aside.

I caught Jo's attention and asked for eggs and toast, with another order of the same packaged to go. Rusty had been pretty patient this morning and he deserved a little extra treat.

"Late night, I guess," I said to Michaela.

She tilted her gray head in a small nod.

"Any idea who caused Amanda's accident?"

"Not yet," she said, her voice a little tight. A stranger showing up in town and questioning her police work wasn't setting well. "I'll get over to Woody's and look at the vehicle in a little bit. Got pictures last night but it was too dark to tell much."

I could tell her that it was a high-sitting red vehicle but decided to keep my mouth shut. She wasn't the kind of woman who wanted advice, and I imagined that extended into other aspects of her life besides her job, too.

"Those kids," she said, "If it's not one thing, it's another."

"Kids?"

"Amanda and Jake. Not going to be easy on them, replacing the vehicle. I'm sure they won't get enough of a settlement to help any."

I glanced at the surrounding tables. Two were empty now and at the third were a group of construction workers who were totaling up their bill and getting ready to leave. I leaned in closer to Michaela.

"Financial problems?" I asked.

"The usual stuff young couples get into today. Credit cards, second mortgages."

My eyebrows must have raised a notch.

"Mary Beth over at the title company is my neighbor. They did a second mortgage a couple months ago to cover some credit card stuff, that's all."

I guess there's something to be said for living in a big, impersonal city where you don't know any of your neighbors. I wrestled between the ethics of listening to gossip versus learning all I could about my client. But it turned out not to matter. Michaela drained the last of her coffee, patted the table top, and stood up.

"Gotta go," she said. "Lots to do today."

I poked at the scrambled eggs on my plate. The diner had almost cleared and Jo finished ringing up a sale then came around again with the coffee pot.

I motioned her to sit when she got to my table. With an eye toward who might overhear, I asked, "Who do you know that drives a red pickup around here? Or maybe a red Suburban or something big like that?"

She leaned back in her chair, taking a couple of minutes because it obviously felt good to be off her feet. Her reddish brows knitted and she blew a puff of breath upward, fluffing her bangs for a second.

"Gosh, hadn't really thought about it," she said. "Lot of trucks around here. You might have noticed from outside." She tilted her head toward the parking area, which had largely cleared by now. But it was true, the lot had been full of trucks just a half hour ago.

The tiny bell at the door tinkled and she turned, ready to rise for a new customer. The stringy guy with long hair wore a sleeveless black T-shirt with some kind of heavy-metal band logo on it. Jo pulled herself to her feet and picked up her carafe.

"That guy's brother has a red truck," she whispered, leaning close to me.

"Who's he?"

"Billy Rodman."

Rodman, Rodman. "Rocko Rodman?"

"That's Rocko," she said, tilting her head toward the newcomer who had taken a seat at the counter. Her voice dropped to a slight whisper. "Had a rock band when he was a teenager." She rolled her eyes. "No, it's his brother, Billy, who has the truck."

She scooted off to pour him some coffee and to cash out another customer. I spread jelly on my toast and watched Rocko's back as he gave Jo his order and stared up at the TV set in the corner. His voice sounded polite as he exchanged a little banter with Jo. He said please and thank you, and despite his rough appearance seemed a nice enough guy. I lingered with another cup of coffee and my final piece of toast, watching for a sign of a guy who would fly into a jealous rage over his girlfriend, but it didn't come out while I was looking.

He whipped through a plate of bacon and eggs, wiped his mouth and paid his bill. A fine, upstanding citizen. I watched him walk out the door and climb onto a Harley. It roared out of the lot as I gathered Rusty's to-go meal and paid for everything.

Out in the car, it took some effort but I managed to convince Rusty to wait until we'd gotten back to the motel before opening the container with his breakfast in it. Although the journey was less than half a block, the anticipation was killing him. I paid—drops of doggy drool spotted my car seats by the time we arrived. I opened the box on the porch of our cabin and let him go at it. In less time than the drive over from Jo's, he'd polished off every scrap.

As I picked up the food box and headed toward the trash basket inside, I wondered about Rocko and whether there was some connection between his brother's truck and last night's incident. There must be.

The beauty of a small town phone directory is that few people go to the trouble or expense to get unlisted numbers, the way they do in a big city—strange, because aren't you a lot more anonymous when at least a dozen other people share your last name? But at any rate, Billy Rodman was listed and I matched the address with the one Michaela had given me yesterday, on one of the town's little side streets. A cruise-by wouldn't hurt, would it?

Rusty wasn't thrilled by the idea of getting right back into the car, but I wasn't going to leave him on his own at the motel.

"It won't take long, I promise."

He balked when I opened the back door for him and I spotted his leash on the back seat.

"Okay, okay. A walk would do us both good." I retrieved the leash and clipped it to his collar. He immediately perked up.

A woman and her dog, out for a walk. Now that couldn't draw too much attention, could it? We followed the main street for three blocks, then turned right. For the first time, I noticed a little bookstore on the corner and promised myself that I would get back there before my visit was over. Rusty managed to sniff every shrub and flower pot along the way but he was thoughtful enough not to yank my arm off in the process.

One block north of Main Street, we made a left turn and found ourselves on Quarter Horse Road, a side street of depressing little houses with short chain link fences around their small front yards. The Rodman house was number twelve and I managed to spot it without any great difficulty. The house was a small box with a pitched roof, two windows and a door showing on the front. Beside it, a detached garage was nearly the same size as the house. Both were painted a deep green with flaky patches revealing the gray wood beneath. The Harley was in the front yard but the place looked otherwise quiet. I gave it a long stare, to be sure it was the same bike, and at that moment the front door opened.

Rocko came out, striding purposefully toward his bike and he caught me looking. He watched me closely and our eyes met for a second. I gave a tiny wave and fell back into woman-out-walking-dog mode. Rusty would have paused for a visit but I firmly pulled him back in line and kept a steady pace to the end of the block.

Behind me I could hear the Harley rumble to life and felt the ground quiver as it passed me. Rocko didn't look back. I turned right at the next corner and aurally followed his progress in the opposite direction.

Rusty and I circled the block and found ourselves back on Rodman's street. Well, we knew where Rocko was, didn't we? And we could be pretty sure we'd know if he returned. And there was that garage, just waiting to be explored. I gave a quick glance up and down the narrow dirt street and stepped through the ungated chain link fence.

"Be really quiet," I whispered to Rusty, as if that would make a difference.

The front door of the garage, actually two swinging doors that met in the middle with a large hasp and padlock, looked impenetrable without tools and the cover of darkness, so I walked around to the side. A grimy window was meant to let in light, I felt sure, but it was blocked with stacks of junk inside and was dirty enough to filter out any attempt at effective peering. The back of the building afforded no access at all, so it was the fourth side, the one facing the house that would both interest me and surely be most dangerous.

From the back corner, I glanced toward the house, saw no sign of life, and edged quickly to the walk-in door that connected, via a short sidewalk, to the back door of the house. A quick test showed that it was unlocked, so I twisted the knob and stepped in, pulling the unsuspecting Rusty with me. I silently apologized to him for leading him into this life of crime; it was, after all, his first breaking and entering offense, although it was by no means mine.

The red pickup truck filled most of the space, except for a workbench that ran along the front wall and stacks of boxes along the wall, accounting for the window blockage that thwarted me from outside.

I knew what I was after and I crossed to the right front fender. A long scrape gave testimony to the contact last night with Amanda Zellinger's Blazer. The damage was surprisingly little, considering what hers looked like, and it probably would attract no notice once a layer or two of dirt covered it. The rest of the truck wasn't exactly pristine, with dents and bungles in several places. With the paint sample from Amanda's wreckage, a pretty good case could be built, I guessed. Sheriff Michaela would be glad to know she could wrap this one up quickly.

My smile of self congratulation faded though as a distinctive sound began to register, coming from outside. The Harley.

My stomach did a big lurch and I dashed to the side door. Through the glass in its top panel, I saw Rocko dismount and pull a small grocery sack from his saddlebag. He looked up, toward the front door of the house, and exchanged words with someone. A second later, another man—a larger, if better dressed, version of Rocko—stepped off the front porch and headed toward the garage, a ring of keys dangling from his fingers.

Shit!

Rocko went into the house and the padlock on the front of the garage began to rattle.

A low growl rumbled in Rusty's throat and I shushed him before he decided to bellow forth with raucous barking.

"Hush," I cautioned. My mind went into overdrive. There was no innocent explanation for my being here. Sorry, I'm a stranger in town and just got lost. No, it wasn't going to work. I heard the padlock leave the hasp and the hasp grind back with a small squeak.

Was Rocko in the house at this moment, standing at the kitchen window, putting his groceries away? My odds probably favored exactly that. Meanwhile, Billy began pushing one of the doors aside and light streaked into the dusty garage. No choice. I grabbed the knob of the side door and pulled it open.

Cinching Rusty's leash in as tightly as I could, I ducked through the door with the dog at my side. Close the door, Charlie. At the last second I did, and in one smooth motion dashed around to the back of the garage building. I leaned against it for a second, remembering to breathe again and hoping like hell that no windows of the house looked out this direction. A cautious glance assured me that I was, at least temporarily, out of sight.

The relief was shattered a moment later when I heard a shout, disturbingly close.

"Billy!" Rocko must be standing on the back porch. He couldn't be more than twenty feet from me right now.

Rusty's growl started again and I reached down to touch him on the muzzle.

I'm dead, I'm dead, I thought.

But Rocko's shout was answered from the front part of the garage.

"What?"

"Your boss is on the phone."

"Tell him I left five minutes ago."

I held my breath, hoping that would be the extent of the conversation. When the truck roared to life a minute later, I breathed again. I bided my time until he backed out, tapped my toe while I listened to him go back and close the garage doors, and relaxed slightly as the truck drove off down the road. I glanced toward the house and finally risked a peek toward the back of it. The door was closed again and I could faintly hear the sounds of a television set.

"Okay, let's play this cool," I said to Rusty.

We circled the garage and made our way out the gap in the fence without being yelled at, jumped, or shot. At the street again, I resumed my dog-walking role, taking the direction that would get me back to the motel the fastest.

My heartbeat managed to return to normal after the close call at the Rodman house, although the altitude was still doing a number on my breathing. I puffed my way up the final incline and noticed that even Rusty had slowed down. We got to the room and both partook of long drinks of water.

I dialed the sheriff's office, hoping in a way that Michaela wouldn't be there and that I could simply leave a message suggesting that she take a look at Billy Rodman's vehicle. The sheriff had already dropped the hint that she wasn't especially keen on my presence here in town.

"Sheriff's department, can I help you?" It came out as 'kina hep ya' in a high female voice of indeterminate age.

I asked for Michaela and was informed that 'she's gone downta lake.' I left a message with the information about the red truck.

"She ain't gonna get this real soon," the receptionist said. "They're pulling a car out."

chapter

9

S he would have been willing to go on, speculating all day long, but I could tell after a couple of questions that she really didn't know more than she'd already told me. I thanked her and hung up.

"This could get interesting," I told Rusty.

I grabbed a jacket and my purse and his leash. He eagerly preceded me to the Jeep and hopped up into the back seat.

The highway curved around the lake on two sides, north and west, the east side being bordered by forest and the south open to the natural valley between two ranges of mountains. A dam, built in the early twentieth century, blocked the water at its narrow point, and formed the deepest part of the lake. Winter snows and spring rains normally kept the water level stable, but we'd had three years of drought conditions. The dry seasons provided my husband with work, I had to admit, but they also changed conditions for all the lakes and rivers statewide. Along the edge of Watson's Lake, a clear border showed that the waterline was at least twenty feet lower than normal, I noticed as I cruised slowly along the road watching for signs of activity.

There were only three or four little roads leading off the highway toward the lake, but I wasn't familiar enough with the area to know which one to take. Michaela could be any-where, including somewhere out in the middle on a boat. About the time I'd decided to just start guessing, an ambulance roared past me. This being what investigators call a clue, I sped up and followed it.

It turned off at the marina road and bumped its way over the washboarded gravel road. I dropped back to avoid flying rocks and a faceful of dust. At the marina—loosely named such because it consisted of only a little convenience store-gas depot and a few rental fishing boats—a uniformed officer waved the ambulance down a secondary road that followed the lake's edge. He stopped me and asked what I was doing here. I introduced myself and saw that my name made no impression on him.

"I was just on the phone with Michaela's office. I have a message for her." All of that was true.

He gave a weary nod and waved me through, not piecing together the fact that any message of importance would have surely come to the sheriff by radio, not via some out-of-town woman civilian. However, I didn't intend to question his laxity and I wasted no time in following the ambulance over a slight rise and down the opposite side, getting myself out of the officer's sight.

The narrow lane served as access to three or four boat ramps, little single-car concrete pads that people used as launching points for their personal boats. The ramps were each about a hundred yards apart, on my left-hand side. On the right, open space provided parking for vehicles and boat trailers. We passed two such ramps and a half-dozen parked, empty trailers before I spotted the cluster of activity at the third ramp. I pulled to the right and parked the Jeep well out of the way.

The sheriff's brown and gold cruiser and now the ambulance were the only vehicles on the boat ramp. A few other vehicles had made it this far, most of them private pickup trucks with removable emergency strobes and Watson's Lake Volunteer Fire Department license plates. I sidestepped through knee-high sage and wild grasses that grew along the road and edged my way through the muddle of people and trucks. Woody's tow truck sat beside the road, beyond the ramp. I spotted Woody himself at the edge of the hubbub, hands in pockets, staring out over the water.

"What's going on?" I asked him.

"Car in the water," he said. "Me and a fisherman found it 'while ago."

"Really? Somebody overshoot the ramp?"

He shrugged. "Could be. Did it a long time ago, though. Car's been in there awhile."

It took some doing but I finally pulled out the details. Woody and a customer had been fishing about twenty yards offshore, right where the water depth drops off quite a bit. The man, 'some damn fool city dude,' got a very expensive lure snagged on something and was ready to jump into the water to retrieve it. When Woody steered the boat in closer it bumped something hard under the water. The customer— 'acted like he thinks he's Indiana Jones or something'— jumped in to unhook the lure and found himself standing on the hood of a car.

"Damn thing was barely submerged," Woody said.

"Do they know how it got there?"

His steady stare let me know what a stupid question that was. "Well, ma'am—" dumb city-slicker lady "—I'd guess he drove it in." He relaxed the put-down tone in his voice. "People do that. Go to back their boats in, don't quite know when to stop. Trailer gets rolling, won't stop, whole car goes in. Ground drops off pretty quick out there."

"But wouldn't the guy just have it towed out? I mean, surely he wouldn't just go off and abandon his car."

Woody shrugged. "Too embarrassed to report it? Water's always been real deep here. Maybe he thought they'd never get it out."

Or the other awful possibility. The guy went down with the car. The ambulance's flashing lights finally registered with me; that must be exactly what had happened.

One of the volunteer firemen came over and got into

a discussion with Woody about whether the fishing was any good lately. I left them and edged closer to the boat ramp, watching Michaela in action. She looked less grandmotherly than ever as she directed a couple of divers in dry suits and scuba gear. I couldn't hear their words, but it looked as if the divers had already been down, were passing on some information, and were now being directed to go back.

Michaela stepped to the back of the ambulance and spoke to the paramedics. They opened the back doors and lifted a stretcher out. I felt my stomach twist.

At the water's edge, the two divers were walking slowly up the ramp, progress made awkward by their rubber swim fins and by the heavy burden they were struggling with. An unrecognizable lump, six feet long and draped in soggy, muddy clothing, was all I could see. I stared in horrified fascination as they dragged it through the bobbing wavelets, where someone had spread out a black bag on the edge of the concrete. They flopped the lump onto the center of the body bag and zipped it quickly inside. The paramedics got it onto their stretcher, shoved it into the ambulance, and slammed the doors in under two minutes. I turned aside in fear of losing my breakfast.

"You're looking a little green there, girl." Michaela had apparently spotted me on the way to find Woody.

She called out to him and he headed for his tow truck.

"Looks like you've got the answer to your question," she said to me.

My face must have registered the blankness inside my head.

"I suspected it from the description of the car," she said, nodding toward the lake. "But the tag numbers confirmed it. That was David Simmons."

She walked away.

I got a peculiar hollow sensation, like the air had been sucked out of the atmosphere and I was standing a great distance away, watching the whole scene down a long tunnel.

Woody's truck backed down the ramp and one of the divers took a cable. Minutes later, or maybe it was hours—I couldn't be sure—the line came winching upward with a red car attached. The red convertible that several residents had sworn was seen driving out of town four years ago. I swallowed hard and walked over to Michaela's cruiser where she was saying something into her radio microphone.

"Amanda," I said when she finished. "Has anyone told Amanda yet?"

"Not yet. That's usually my job. Not the fun part." She gave me a straight stare.

"You want me to do it?" My voice squeaked a little.

She sighed and shook her head. "Not yet. We better make sure. All we know right now is that it's his car. We'll get the M.E. right on it, though. You could go sit with Amanda, if you would. Could go ahead and tell her about the car—only the car. When we do get the call, it would be easier for her if she's had a little warning, a friend to be there with her. Earleen's also going to have to get the news."

"I'll take Amanda," I said.

Michaela could have Earleen any day. She gave me a wry grin that let me know she'd precisely read my thoughts.

All of us watched somberly as Woody winched the scum-covered car onto his truck, tightened everything down, and prepared to drive away. The news would be filtering through town by now and I decided Michaela was right. Amanda would need a friend right now.

I arrived at her front door in time to hear the phone ringing inside. I clenched my teeth, hoping it would be a wrong number. The ringing stopped and Amanda's voice responded.

"No!" she screamed, the word coming through clearly.

I twisted the knob and was relieved when it opened. I stepped inside, calling her name softly. She was in the living room, standing beside the blanket-strewn sofa, the phone to her ear. Tears ran down her face and her gaze darted furiously around the room as if looking for a way she could escape the words from the telephone. I stepped over to her and reached out. She slumped into my arms and I barely caught the receiver before it dropped to the floor.

"Thanks for calling but Amanda can't handle this right now," I said quickly and clicked off the call.

I helped her to sit on the sofa and she collapsed against me. The phone immediately rang again, but we both ignored it.

"At this point they've only identified the car," I told her. "Sheriff Michaela said the medical examin—"

"It's him, I know it is," she wailed. "It's why he never called. It's—"

I patted her back, feeling awkward, not knowing what else to do or say.

The phone quit ringing, then immediately started again. I set Amanda back against the cushions and reached for the phone. "Is there a way to turn off the ringer on this thing?" I asked.

She stared helplessly at it, not even comprehending my question. I fiddled with it for another minute and found a small switch that did the trick. The phone had no sooner gone quiet than the wireless intercom, which I'd left for her earlier on the coffee table, crackled with a staticky version of Jake's voice.

"Amanda, what's going on in there? Why's the phone ringing?"

I pressed the Talk button. "Jake, it's Charlie. You better come in here."

Two minutes later, the back door opened roughly and his footsteps crossed the kitchen. "What the hell—I'm trying to get some work done out there," he said.

Amanda went into a fresh series of violent sobs and I shot Jake a look of pure impatience. His demeanor switched instantly.

"Honey?" he crossed to the couch and sat on the other side of her, letting her collapse against him.

"They found her father's car in the lake," I said softly.

His face drained of color.

"We don't know for a fact that it's David, but it kind of looks that way. People have been calling. I guess the news is getting around."

Jake pulled his wife to him and cupped his hand around her face. I left them that way and found a bathroom just off the kitchen. After I'd used the facilities for my own purposes, I dampened a washcloth with cool water and filled a glass for Amanda. Back in the living room she had quieted and I offered the small comforts I'd brought. Jake seemed distracted so I waved him away and he seemed grateful to get back to his lab.

"He wasn't always this way," she said. "Jake and I were really close in the early years. When we first moved here it was nearly perfect." Her expression became soft. "The last few years . . . I don't know."

I thought of Michaela's comment about their money worries.

Amanda dabbed at her face, but the stitches and blackened eyes were still painful.

"Can I get you some more of your painkillers?" I asked, taking a seat in the recliner by the sofa.

She shook her head and wiped her nose on the cloth. "I'll be okay," she mumbled nasally.

"Anything from the kitchen?" I felt at a loss for what to do next. I'm not very adept at dealing with people's emotions.

She looked at me sympathetically and I got the feeling she was thinking up a small task for me so I wouldn't continue to watch her so awkwardly.

"Tea would be nice," she said. "Everything's on the shelf beside the stove."

I accepted her sympathy much more easily than I was

able to give it. As she'd said, a canister with various flavors of tea was right there on the shelf. A kettle on the stove already contained water. I simply had to turn on the burner. While it began to hiss faintly I found some mugs and unwrapped two of the teabags. In a further stalling measure I poked around in the breadbox and cabinets and found a package of chocolate chip cookies. On the theory that chocolate chip cookies can cure virtually anything, I grabbed them. A decorative bamboo tray helped me carry off the illusion that I could play perfect caregiver, tending to the needs of my wounded charge.

Amanda had recovered somewhat when I came back. I'd remembered to put sugar and milk on the tray, but she took the tea pure black.

"When . . . when will they. . ."

"I don't know. Michaela said the M.E.'s office would run some tests. Pretty soon, I'd guess."

"Did you see . . ."

"Not really," I said. "I was there, but you couldn't see much. The paramedics were very professional." Somehow I sensed that she was reassured by this, some little knowledge that her father's body hadn't been treated badly, been an object of disrespect.

She drained her tea and refused my offer to get more.

"I should go there," she said, rising. "To see him."

I shrank from the idea and it must have showed on my face.

"I'll take Jake's car and go by myself," she said. "You don't need to come."

"Amanda . . ." I got up as she winced in pain. "Look, you shouldn't be driving. Every muscle in your body hurts. Let me take you."

"I'll just—just get dressed." Her breath grabbed as she began to move but she waved away my attempt to brace her. She hobbled away and the bedroom door closed.

Where would they have taken the body, I wondered.

In a town of five or six hundred people, was there a morgue or hospital? I hadn't seen anything like that. When Amanda came out ten minutes later, dressed in gray sweats and a baggy top, I asked her. She'd pulled her hair back into a ponytail, making no attempt to cover the bruises on her face, ready to show them boldly to anyone who dared to stare.

"I'm not sure," she said, pausing to think about it. She picked up the telephone and dialed a number from memory. "This is Amanda Zellinger," she said in a firm voice. "I want to talk to Sheriff Michaela. However you need to reach her."

A few minutes of silence went by, followed by a short greeting on Amanda's part and a few uh-huhs and all rights. She hung up and moaned as she attempted to slip a jacket on.

"You're in no shape to drive," I said. "Tell me where we're going and I'll take you there."

"The clinic. It's near the community center."

I used the intercom box to tell Jake where we were going, then took Amanda's elbow and made sure she was steady on her feet as we went out to the car. The fact of a big reddish-brown dog in the back seat startled her and I ordered him to back away. Luckily, he actually did so.

She directed me as to which turns to make and we pulled up in front of an unimposing one-story wooden building with a steeply pitched red-metal roof. Apparently when necessary the county medical examiner worked from the small clinic that normally handled sniffles and the occasional broken arm. Michaela's cruiser sat out front, along with a couple of other vehicles.

Amanda unclicked her seatbelt the moment we stopped and was out the door before I'd shut off the engine. I hoped she wouldn't go barging into a scene that could easily traumatize anyone; the sight of a body that had been underwater for four years couldn't be a good one.

Luckily, Michaela met us at the door and took Amanda firmly by the arm. "Come here and sit down," she ordered, leading Amanda into the waiting room. I followed but left them a little space.

"We're getting the ID on the . . . the subject now," Michaela said.

Amanda's eyes welled and her lips clamped together, but she nodded and managed not to break down.

"Sit here," Michaela said, directing the younger woman to a chair and guiding her into it. "I'm going to be back very shortly."

I scooted over and sat in the adjoining chair before Amanda could make a move to disobey.

Michaela disappeared down a corridor, but true to her word she came back within five minutes. She carried a large brown envelope and strode purposefully toward us. Behind her, Earleen and Frank trailed along, Earleen whining something about her rights.

Michaela turned on her and said something low and sharp. The grieving widow stopped and blinked, her mouth working up and down but not coming out with anything. I admired the sheriff's way with words.

"Come on, babe," said Frank. "We're getting out of here." He took her arm and practically yanked her toward the door.

I sent a questioning glance toward the sheriff. She approached Amanda, told her Earleen had identified David's belongings, and offered condolences. Then she held out the brown envelope.

"Your father's personal effects. We found a note saying he wanted you to have them."

I remembered how, amazingly, documents can sometimes survive in cold water, as many had in the wreckage of Titanic. The body itself probably hadn't fared so well. Temperatures and water had to have done their job, not to mention the little fishies. I forced my mind to other things.

Amanda broke down again and buried her face against Michaela's ample chest. Stiffly, the sheriff handed the envelope to me and put both arms around the girl. She let Amanda sob for a couple of minutes then started to make parting noises. Michaela handed her over to me, gave me a nod, and indicated that she needed to get back to the other room. I placed the envelope in Amanda's hands and she hugged it to her as if it were a warm teddy bear.

"I can stay with you awhile," I said as I tucked her into the passenger's seat.

She nodded numbly.

"Can you eat anything? It would be a good idea." I'd had the idea of stopping along the way and getting some chicken or something to take home.

She shook her head, the same blank expression on her face.

"Okay. We'll deal with food later."

Back at the house, Jake was still tucked away in his lab and Amanda seemed grateful that I'd offered to stay with her. I wondered at his detachment. In Amanda's time of grief she needed him. And what about his own feelings about David, their work together? I guessed seclusion was simply his way of dealing with it.

Amanda had put the envelope on the coffee table and curled herself into a tight ball of pain on the sofa, her blanket wrapped snugly around her.

"You sure I can't get you anything?" I asked. I felt like my role here should be some kind of cross between Martha Stewart and June Cleaver, dispensing care and comfort while the whole mess magically cleaned itself up and life became pretty again. "You haven't eaten anything all day, have you?" I asked.

She shook her head and mumbled something about not being hungry. June Cleaver would have never accepted that answer and while I wasn't quite ready to make chicken soup the Martha way, by first killing a live chicken, I could at least locate a can of Campbell's and get some bit of nourishment into my new charge.

By the time I'd managed to find everything I needed in the kitchen, she'd cried herself out temporarily and I got her to sit up with a tray on her lap and consume some soup and crackers. Her bruises were looking worse, brilliant purple-black now, and she requested more pain medicine. Within ten minutes her eyelids looked heavy. I removed the lunch tray and when I came back from the kitchen she was out cold.

The brown envelope called out to me. At first I resisted, knowing that Amanda should be the first to go through it, or should at least give her consent before I opened it. But she was so tired . . . and I wasn't going to take anything. It would still be waiting for her when she woke up.

"AmandacanIlookthroughthis?" I whispered.

She snored lightly and burrowed deeper into the blanket.

"Thanks." Okay, I know that really wasn't permission in the traditional sense. But let's don't argue semantics. I picked up the envelope and quickly undid the metal clasp. A wave of musty, damp smell came up at me and I decided to take it to the kitchen table.

Someone had made an effort to dry the items but there was the desolate sense of drowning and abandonment when I dumped everything onto the table. A man's wallet—the leather soggy and pliable, a gold watch—amazingly intact and still ticking, a ring of keys, a simple gold wedding band and a signet ring with a large round ruby that must have been a joy to retrieve. I gave the jewelry a quick look but couldn't dwell too long on the image of the waterlogged flesh they'd come from.

The key ring must have been pulled from the car's ignition. It held one automobile key, three that looked like house keys, and an odd one that I could swear went to a bank's safe deposit box. I stuck the keys in my pocket, thinking I'd ask Amanda if one of them belonged to her house or the lab, and if she knew anything about a safe deposit box.

The wallet was of the most interest, still containing credit cards and driver's license, which identified David Simmons. I looked at the photo of him. The laminate had held and the picture was as clear as if it had been taken last week, a serious-looking blond man of—I calculated his age—fifty-one. Well, he'd be fifty-one now. He'd been around forty-five when the picture was taken, a handsome guy whose charisma managed to show even in a routine DMV photo.

A small ID card with "In Case of Emergency Call" was filled out with Amanda's name. Curious, why his daughter instead of his wife, but that was undoubtedly the 'note' Michaela had referred to when she bypassed Earleen in favor of Amanda earlier. The wallet also contained twelve dollars in cash and a few other IDs, insurance, health plan, and all that. Twelve dollars wasn't much for a man who intended to set a fire and disappear.

Michaela must have inventoried these possessions before handing them over. I wondered if she was thinking the same thing I was thinking.

I picked up the kitchen phone and dialed her office. The same receptionist who had offered to 'hep' me earlier informed me that the sheriff was out on business. I left my cell phone number and asked that she call me as soon as she could.

I'd no sooner gone back into the living room to get my purse and retrieve then cell phone then it rang. I answered in a whisper and carried it out the front door, not wanting to disturb Amanda's nap.

"Michaela Fritz, returning your call."

"Hi, Sheriff. I'm at Amanda's. She's napping at the moment and I had a question about the contents of David's wallet."

"Might as well hold on to it. I'll be out there in about thirty minutes." She clicked off before I could say anything else.

Poor Rusty panted out the side window and I felt a pang

that he'd had to spend so much time today in the car. I let him out and gave him free run of the woods until Michaela's cruiser pulled into the drive. Rusty bounded up to greet her but settled onto the front porch within a couple of minutes.

"So, what's the big question?" she asked as we walked toward the house.

"Twelve dollars in Simmons's wallet. Doesn't seem like much for a guy to live on if he plans to be out of town for awhile. I know lots of people use credit cards for everything these days, but that wouldn't have been feasible if he planned to hide out, would it?"

"Doesn't seem like it to me," she said. "Guess I looked through all his stuff but hadn't really pieced it all together yet."

She paused on the front step. "Before we go in . . . I'm here to deliver bad news."

Worse than the shocks Amanda had already received today?

"That was no accident, David being in the lake. Preliminary autopsy showed blunt force trauma to the back of the skull. And, based on where we found the car, somebody sent the vehicle into the water at a pretty good rate of speed. Rigged the gas pedal somehow, is my guess, but we'll know more about that later. The car sat in nearly twenty feet of water all this time. If we hadn't had this drought it still would be. Lake hasn't been this low in fifty years or more. Pure chance that fisherman bumped into it."

"Any way to know how long David's been dead?"

She shook her head. "Cold water, that amount of time. Can't really say. Has to be nearly the whole four years, but no way to know if it happened the same day of the fire or a month later. Just can't be that precise at this point."

"Does Amanda need to know all this?" I asked. "She's pretty shaken up already."

"I have to tell her we're changing the focus of our investigation. If David rigged the gas explosion, then who killed him? Bettina's death might have been an accident, but this, this is obviously murder. State police are probably going to get their noses into it, too." She said this last part with a small curl of the lip. "I'm going to need that envelope back, David's personal effects."

We let ourselves into the house and I offered to get the envelope from the kitchen while she talked to Amanda. When I came back into the living room, Amanda was sitting on the edge of the sofa and Michaela perched on the edge of a chair, their knees almost touching.

"I'm sorry that all the old questions are going to come up again," the sheriff said.

Amanda rubbed at her face but her eyes were dry. "It's okay. I want the answers. I have to know who did this."

Michaela stood and I handed her the brown envelope. The unpleasant part was over for her. She could make her announcement and walk out the door, go home for a nice dinner. Amanda's nightmare would go on for a long time.

chapter

⇥11⇤

The sun was low in the sky and I was more than ready for some solitude. Shortly after Michaela left the Zellinger house Jake came in and I left Amanda in his capable hands. It had been an intense day and I wanted nothing more than a walk in the fresh air and a simple dinner.

I parked in front of our rustic little cabin at the Horseshoe and turned Rusty loose in the wide open space behind it. I walked the perimeter of the big field, enjoying the sunset and hoping that Drake would be able to call tonight. I missed our daily contact when he was away on jobs. After thirty minutes of fast walking I felt better. The sun had gone behind the mountain and the temperature had dropped ten degrees. We walked up to Jo's where I ordered a salad to go.

Back in the room I switched on the television and ate my salad, but neither the food or the sitcom could distract me from the rush of random thoughts about the case. When Drake called he sounded tired and we covered the basics of the day and ended with our usual love-you, miss-you. I'd told him about David's body being recovered and he sounded relieved because that would be the end of my involvement. And it probably should be. I should just check out of the motel in the morning and go back to Albuquerque. There were surely letters to be written and bills to be paid back at the office.

I pulled off my jeans and T-shirt. A shower would feel really good. When I tossed the jeans over the back of the desk's straight chair, something hit the floor. I went over to check.

David's key ring.

I'd forgotten all about having put it in my pocket. I'd been meaning to ask Amanda to identify the keys when she woke up. Now that the sheriff had the envelope back, she'd surely check the contents and notice the keys were missing. Oh boy.

A slew of thoughts hammered me—my culpability in hiding evidence or obstructing an investigation or some such thing. I glanced at the telephone. Should I call Michaela and explain? Should I tell Amanda? I fingered the keys, again wondering whether any of them provided actual evidence.

Maybe not. Maybe they were simply keys. House, car, the usual. Safe deposit box. People put valuable and secret things in safe deposit boxes. I jammed the keys back into the jeans pocket and headed toward the shower.

While I soaped and shampooed, I wondered what to do next. I couldn't see that anything could be accomplished tonight. I would get the keys over to the sheriff first thing in the morning. If I slept on it, some kind of explanation would come to me.

As it turned out, I didn't sleep on it all that well. It's never a good idea to go to bed with a guilty secret and mine seemed compounded by all the questions about both the explosion and David's murder, by all the alibis and suspects that seemed to be everywhere. Somewhere in the early hours of the morning I drifted into a sleep of restless and disturbing dreams, the kind of dreams that feel disjointed and anxious. I woke about five and lay there in the tangled sheets, wondering what time the bank opened.

There was no way around it. I had to find out what was in that box before simply handing over the keys to the sheriff. I would probably be in deep shit for doing it, but I'd deal with that when it happened.

I paced the room, took another shower, and dressed in the same pair of jeans, checking to be sure the keys were still in the pocket. The air was frosty again this morning, with clouds starting to build on the western horizon. Rusty nosed at the rimed blades of grass and would have probably done so all day, but I finally called him back.

The bank probably wouldn't open until nine and the suspense was killing me. I opened the book I'd brought and read the same two sentences over and over as I alternately looked at the clock and wondered when Sheriff Michaela would come pounding on the door.

The more I thought about it, the more I realized that I wasn't simply going to be able to walk into the bank, a stranger in town, and get into David's box. A relative would have to do it and that meant either Amanda or Earleen. No way was I calling Earleen. I dialed Amanda's number and got a sleepy response.

"I'm so sorry to call this early," I told her, realizing I'd done the same thing on the previous morning as well. "I need to check out something at your dad's bank this morning and, well, I need your help."

Her voice brightened. Helping, I realized, was just the thing Amanda needed right now. Doing something is always better than lying around and waiting for news.

"Jake must already be out in the lab," she said. "What time is it?"

"Six thirty. I know it's way early for the bank. Maybe we could meet for breakfast and then go over there?"

She hesitated.

"I'm sorry. You probably don't want to be out in public too much, do you?"

"These black eyes would terrify my students if any of them were to see me. How about you come out here to the house? I'll get a shower and try to become presentable, we'll make breakfast here, and then we can go to the bank."

I found it amazing that she didn't ask more questions about the nature of this banking business, but was just as glad to save the explanation as to why I had her father's keys when I'd turned everything else over to the law. I told her I'd be there in thirty minutes.

When I tapped on their door, Jake answered. He looked fresh and vital, wearing a white lab coat. He ushered me in and we walked through the kitchen where Amanda was just taking a tray of bacon from the microwave. Jake took two strips of it and headed out the back door, toward the lab.

"He's not much of a breakfast person?" I asked.

"Hardly ever. He's already been out there at work since before daylight." She sighed and put the final stir on a skillet full of scrambled eggs and scooped them onto two waiting plates. I watched as she carried them to the table and pressed the lever on the toaster. Her face looked better today, as some of the smaller bruises had begun to fade. She still moved a bit cautiously but more fluidly than yesterday.

We buttered the toast and dug into the food before saying much more. Finally, she paused and set her fork down. I knew the time for explanation had come.

"I have to start out with an apology," I told her. She gave a quizzical look and I continued. "I looked through your father's things yesterday, while you were sleeping."

"The envelope?"

"Yeah." The words came out in a rush. "I should have waited for you, I know, but now that Michaela's taken them away again . . ."

"Tell me. What did you find?"

I briefly described the wallet's contents and the jewelry before I mentioned the key ring. Then I pulled it out of my pocket.

"Do you know anything about a safe deposit box?" I asked.

A wrinkle creased her forehead as she thought about it. "At the National State Bank branch here in town." She flipped through the keys and came to the one I'd noticed. "Years ago, he made me a signatory on the box, just in case . . ." Her voice trailed off and she didn't finish the thought. "I'd forgotten all about it."

"Can you still get into it?"

"I'm pretty sure I can. He'd given me a key." She got up and rummaged through a kitchen drawer that bristled with junk. After a minute or two she held up a key with a small paper tag on it.

"Does anyone else have one of those?" I leveled a straight gaze at her.

Her mouth opened and she froze. "Earleen?"

I shrugged. "Maybe."

She stared off at a faraway spot and let out her pent-up breath. "I can see why you want to get down there right away." She forked up a clump of scrambled eggs and began chewing furiously.

"I have no idea what we might find, but if there's a chance that we can find it first, I'd like to," I told her.

She nodded.

"When was the last time you opened the box?" I asked as we watched the clock.

"Never. I was with him the only time I ever saw it," she said. "Like I said, he added me to the signature card but I actually saw the box only once."

"Do you know what was in there?"

"Important papers, I guess. I can't recall his ever telling me anything specific."

We lingered with extra cups of coffee and washed the dishes and finally it was a quarter of nine. She clicked the intercom box and told Jake she'd be gone for awhile.

We arrived at the bank in time to see the manager unlock the front door. Amanda greeted the woman by name and received a few condolences on both her father's death and her recent accident. I hung back, and the process of signing the card and unlocking the box with Amanda's key went without a hitch. The manager, introduced to me only as Susan, escorted Amanda into a cubicle and allowed me inside at Amanda's request.

The box was not a large one, probably only about six inches square by eighteen inches long. Amanda lifted the lid and pulled out a stack of folded documents. She quickly unfolded and glanced at each one: an insurance policy, a will, a letter with her name scrawled across the back side. She unfolded this and read through it quickly.

"Oh my gosh." It came out in a whisper.

I itched to look over her shoulder but restrained myself.

"He was divorcing Earleen. Look." She thrust the letter into my hands. It was dated the first of May, four years ago.

> *Dear Amanda,*
>
> *I'll soon be telling you this myself, but in case there's ever a dispute about the conversation, I want to put this in writing. I'm filing for divorce, this week. Horton Blythe is handling it.*

"Horton Blythe?"

"Dad's lawyer. He's in Segundo."

> *In case Earleen tries to drag out the process, I'm doing everything I can to cut her off financially. The enclosed life insurance policy names you as beneficiary and my will has been revised to reflect the same. She married me only for my money, I can see that now. I know, I was foolish about her. The YA-30 research is going well and I think it's going to eventually make all of us very, very wealthy. I just want to be sure Earleen is out of the picture before the real money comes rolling in. Whatever else happens, Amanda, you'll be taken care of.*

He'd signed off with love and reassurances that Amanda would probably never need to deal with any of this as the divorce would be finalized well before the new invention made it to market.

Amanda took everything from the box and stuffed it into her purse.

I found a dozen new possibilities flying through my head. Had David indeed set up the gas explosion, hoping to catch Earleen in it, not realizing that Bettina would get there first?

We stepped out of the cubicle and Amanda handed the box back to Susan.

"Did you also want to look at your father's other box?" she asked.

Amanda went blank. "Other . . .?"

I nudged her and held up David's key ring as it dawned on me that the two keys were evidently not the same.

"Yes, please."

Susan pulled the signature card and I was sure this was the moment she'd realize Amanda knew nothing about this second box, but she merely glanced at it and filed it back in its place.

She pulled a key from the ring on her wristband and opened another box.

"There you go," she said, showing us back to the cubicle.

"What do you suppose this is all about?" Amanda asked, her fingers lingering before raising the lid.

I shrugged.

She pulled at the lid, tentatively, as if something might jump out.

It jumped out at me, all right. A bright flash of gold caught my eye and I recognized the emblematic seal against the dark blue of a U.S. passport. The thing that jumped out was the fact that there were three more of them.

⊰12⊱

Four passports, four Social Security numbers, four identities.

Amanda fumbled with the documents, as if she were unsure what she was seeing. I knew what I was seeing, I just wasn't sure why. The implications became huge.

David's picture was in each of the passports but none of the names was Simmons. Social Security cards, all looking brand new, matched the four identities. Driver's licenses—issued in four different states—matched the other documents. A credit card went along with each, as well. It looked to me like David was prepared to establish himself under a new name in a new place, at any time. Why, then, didn't he use one of these to disappear after the fire? We'd never have been able to track a name we knew nothing about.

If we'd found this box before the car was retrieved yesterday, I would have believed that's exactly what happened. There could have been five false identities, just as easily as four. But if that were the case, we wouldn't have found the body with David's true ID.

Then another thought hit me. Was the body really David's? My head began to pound with the implications.

Amanda continued to flip through the documents, a stunned look on her face. She turned to me.

"I don't know either," I said in response to her unspoken question. "But I think we better take all this with us and try to figure it out."

"Here, you take them. I don't want this stuff," she said, shoving a handful at me.

I gathered everything and rechecked the box to be sure it was empty. We walked out, returned the box, and left the bank. Both of us must have looked somewhat shell-shocked.

Out in my car, we sat for a couple of minutes, both staring straight ahead.

"What shall we do?" she finally asked.

"I'm not sure. I think a good first step would be to run backgrounds on all these other names, just see if anything turns up. And I think we better insist that a positive identification is done on the body in the lake."

She sat in frozen silence. A tear trailed down each cheek.

"I'll talk to the sheriff about it, if you want," I said. "You won't have to look at him, you won't have to deal with it. They might just ask you for a DNA sample."

She nodded and the tears continued to roll. Rusty came forward and sniffed at her face, expressing concern in his own doggy way. She smiled and rubbed at his ears.

"Want some coffee?" I finally asked.

She pulled a tissue from her purse, wiped at her face, and blew her nose. With dark glasses, she looked fine for a woman who'd lost her father and been in a car wreck. But she really didn't want to sit in a public place and have people stopping by with their attempts to console her.

"There's a place I love to sit and just think sometimes. If we got coffee to go, we could drive up there."

"Sure." I started the car and pulled out into a short stream of traffic, then turned left two blocks later at Jo's. The stop took just four or five minutes and I handed the two coffees over to

Amanda in the Jeep. Following her directions, ten minutes later we were stopping at a small turnout that overlooked the lake from a height of five or six hundred feet above.

"I'm glad we can't see the boat ramps from here," she said as she took the first sips of her coffee. "I don't think I'm ready for that yet."

I nodded and just let her talk.

"Dad's house was right over there. See the clear spot just above those rocks? You used to look over there and see reflections off the windows sometimes. At night, if the house was lit up, you could see it easily. It was a beautiful place, I have to admit. Even though Earleen hired the decorator, the location and floor plan were Dad's. There was a lot of him in that place. I can't believe—I won't believe—that he had anything to do with destroying it. He was divorcing Earleen anyway, why would he destroy the house he loved so much?"

"Did Earleen know about the divorce?" I asked.

"I have no idea. I didn't. But then he might have wanted to wait and tell me after the papers were served and he knew how she would react." She sipped again at the coffee. "His lawyer would know."

I handed her my cell phone. "Let's find out."

She paged back through the sheets from the first bank box and found the will, which listed Horton Blythe, his office address, and phone number. She got him on the line and asked the question. While she went on to tell Mr. Blythe about yesterday's events, I stepped out of the car and allowed Rusty to run free. When I got back in she had fresh tears on her face.

"I guess I better get used to this," she said. "Everyone's going to be offering condolences."

I waited while she blew her nose again before asking about Earleen.

"Mr. Blythe didn't know for sure. No papers were filed yet, but he didn't know whether Dad had talked to her about it."

A woman scorned. I remembered Earleen's insistence that

she was the legal wife and therefore entitled to any insurance money. If she knew that she would soon no longer be the legal wife, would she have decided to do something about that? If she were going to lose the house anyway would she have destroyed it? Maybe—if she'd arranged the fire to kill David before he could finalize the divorce. If he weren't caught in the explosion she'd have to come up with another way. And maybe she did. Michaela'd said there was no way to tell if the murder happened before or after the fire.

I had a hard time envisioning slender, blonde Earleen actually whacking David over the head, getting him into his car, and managing to get the car into the lake. For one thing, she struck me as the type who'd worry about breaking a nail. But she had dear Frank Quinn in her life. I wondered how long he'd been part of the picture.

I also found myself wondering about the ramifications of the multiple identities. I knew I should immediately turn over every piece of paper we'd found this morning to the authorities, but I held onto the stubborn, vaguely macho idea that I should follow up somehow. That the local authorities would tend to discount them now that they'd found the body and would completely overlook the bigger picture. I caught myself tapping nervously at the steering wheel.

Rusty returned and I let him into the backseat; Amanda finished her coffee and looked to me for a suggestion.

"Is there a copy shop in town?" I asked. "I think we have to turn this stuff over, but I also think it would be a good idea to have copies for our own use."

She thought about it for a minute. "There's a CPA who lets people make copies for a few cents each."

I followed her directions and we got lucky that the copy machine was in a separate alcove where the office staff couldn't get a peek at our business. Once we had legible copies of everything, I faced the inevitable.

"Let's stop by Michaela's," I said.

The sheriff greeted Amanda with a degree of warmth I'd not seen her show yet, and for that I was grateful.

"We found some things in David's safe deposit boxes that may help your investigation," I said after we'd taken seats across the desk from her, handing over the papers and passports.

Michaela paged through them, pausing a moment over the fake identities. "We better do a DNA verification on the . . . uh, subject," she said. She mumbled a bit, thinking aloud about the difficulty of getting hairs or skin cells known to be David's at this late date.

"Amanda's DNA?" I said.

"Guess we'll have to do it that way," she said, groaning as she got up.

She came back a couple of minutes later with a test kit and quickly took a swab sample from Amanda's mouth.

"That's it," she said. "State lab's really backed up, though. Don't know when we'll get a result."

"I'd appreciate anything you can do," Amanda told her.

I drove Amanda home and wondered which direction to go next. She'd left all the copies with me and it seemed like a good idea to take some time to go through them. I arrived back at the motel to discover that the room had been cleaned and there was a message from Ron on the phone. I wondered why he hadn't simply called my cell, but who knew.

As it turned out he was simply wondering when Drake would be home because he'd gotten baseball tickets. I told him he better find someone else to go; Drake might be gone days or weeks.

"But while I have you on the phone . . . more background checks." I gave him the names and data on the four fake names.

"Are we being paid for all this?" he asked, somewhat gruffly.

"You're not over the limit yet," I assured him. I'd pretty well decided that my own time and expenses weren't going to be covered by Amanda's retainer, but we'd get into that later.

Ron told me he'd get back to me with the results of the checks and we hung up.

I boiled water with my handy little coil heater and brewed a cup of tea, spreading David's documents out on the desk. I'd gotten quick glances as we copied them but this was my first chance to read through everything.

The life insurance policy left Amanda pretty well set. A half million dollars. I got to wondering about David's frame of mind at the time he died—suicidal?—but it seemed most likely that he'd simply bought the new policy and named Amanda as beneficiary because he knew he was divorcing Earleen.

The will also seemed to confirm that. It was dated just two weeks before his disappearance and worded carefully to supercede any previous wills. It specifically stated that Earleen Ross Simmons was not to inherit anything. There was also a clause that mentioned a prenuptial agreement, which answered my question about how he was going to get around New Mexico's community property laws.

If Earleen had gotten a hint of this, she may have decided to take what she could get when she could get it. She probably didn't know about the new will or she wanted to act before it went into effect. My money was still on her as the chief suspect.

David's set of fake identities was another matter. I couldn't seem to wrap my mind around that and piece together their purpose. On the face of it, and the conclusion the authorities would probably reach, it looked like David planned to torch his own house, make a getaway, and start a new life with a new identity. And maybe it was just that simple. He'd set up the life insurance for Amanda, knowing that eventually he'd be declared legally dead and she'd have a nest egg to retire on.

But if that were the case, why didn't he simply drive away, without calling attention to himself by exploding the house? The rest of the plan could have worked anyway. My guess was that it was a spiteful move against his wife. If Earleen made it clear that she would make a divorce difficult and miserable, he may have just decided to skip the formality. Leave her with no place to live and let her straighten out the insurance nightmare. In that sense, he had succeeded.

My head began to throb and I realized that I'd eaten nothing since early morning. The facts of this case were not untangling themselves but becoming more muddled the more I thought about them. I needed a break.

I fed Rusty and left him to guard the cabin while I went in search of nourishment for myself. Jo's Café was all right, but I was beginning to tire of the sameness, so I set my sights on Burger Shak, a couple of blocks farther up Main Street. I walked there, setting a brisk pace to help clear the cobwebs from my head. I managed to consume a green chile cheeseburger in fairly record time, along with hand-cut fries and a milkshake made with actual ice cream, not a mix. By the time I set out for the motel I realized that there was no way I could settle down until I'd given myself an hour or two to digest everything.

The tiny bookstore I'd spotted yesterday was still open and I knew it would be easy to while away some time in there. A bell on the door jangled as I went in. Behind the counter a fifty-something guy greeted me distractedly as he fiddled with the tape in his cash register. The place consisted of a series of small rooms with books lining every wall. I bypassed the local history and children's books to find the paperback fiction. My thriller was nearly finished and if I could clear my head enough to concentrate, I'd be needing new reading material soon. I found a mystery by Susan Slater, one of my favorite New Mexico authors, and grabbed it right away. The store's selection was terrific and I kept browsing.

The doorbell made its clinky sound again and I heard the new arrival ask the proprietor if he had any books on winning in Vegas. I wouldn't have paid any attention except that I recognized the voice—Earleen Simmons. I heard the two of them move into the non-fiction room and I kept my back to the doorway connecting the two, so she wouldn't see me.

The store owner suggested a couple of titles and she said she liked the one on winning at craps. "Usually I like blackjack," she said, loudly enough that it was no secret to anyone in the whole building, "but this time I want to try a new game. Frank's promised me a long weekend at the Bellagio."

I didn't hear the man's response but a couple of minutes later the cash register beep-beeped the sale and the door chime signaled her departure.

Vegas, huh. The grieving widow wasn't wasting any time getting on with her life, even before David's funeral. Remembering Michaela's comment, though, about the backup at the state crime lab delaying the DNA test results, I didn't imagine there would be a funeral for awhile. What a tangled mess.

I paid for my books and chatted with the store owner for a few minutes. He turned out to be a friendly guy who knew everyone in town. I filed that for future reference. He'd be a good person to know.

The late afternoon air had cooled quite a bit. I took my time walking back to the motel, clearing my head and looking forward to talking to Drake later. As it turned out I was nearly asleep by the time he called. The heavy dinner and getting to the final chapter of my book had lulled me. We talked about our respective jobs, but mainly focused on how nice it would be to get back home together.

As I drifted off to sleep it struck me that Earleen and Frank were certainly planning an expensive getaway for a couple who seemingly had no money.

⇥13⇤

I slept late and allowed myself the luxury of the warm blankets for a full thirty minutes after my eyes first opened. Eventually, though, my brain zipped through a million thoughts and I couldn't lie still any longer. I brushed my teeth and dressed and walked out back with Rusty, getting a good dose of invigorating mountain air.

I debated about going to Jo's for breakfast. In a lot of ways a muffin from the convenience store and a cup of tea in my room were appealing. Being at home and having a simple breakfast with my neighbor, Elsa, was even more appealing but that was not to be, not just yet. I ended up opting for Jo's and letting Rusty sit outside on her porch while I went in.

The place was crowded again, as I suspected was usual. It clearly served as the gathering spot for the locals. I took a small table near the back and watched people come and go while I waited for my pancakes.

When Earleen and Frank walked in my interest perked. He wore a suit—something that stood out in this town—and he actually cleaned up pretty well. His hair had been freshly cut, and although it was still on the longish side, it now had some style to it. With the tattoos covered, he wasn't a bad looking man. Earleen wore tight spandex leggings and a leopard-spotted top with a flamboyant orange scarf around her neck. They greeted some of the other customers loudly and soon everyone in the place knew they were on their way to Vegas.

"By noon I'll be winning at the craps tables," she told Jo.

"Taking that special Vegas flight out of Segundo?" Jo asked.

"In an hour." Frank dropped his arm possessively around Earleen's shoulders.

They ordered and ate quickly, while I lingered over my short stack and eavesdropped shamelessly. So, where were they getting the money to do this? Earleen might still be under the impression she was going to inherit everything David had, but even if the case went in her favor, she wouldn't see anything for a long time. And if Frank was treating, where did he get the cash?

They called out goodbyes to people as they left and drove away with a happy little toot of the horn.

"Interesting, huh?" said Jo as she refilled my coffee.

"Sounds like they're planning to do it up big," I said.

She shook her head. "I don't know. Didn't think they had that kind of money."

I lowered my voice, which always inspires confidentiality. "So, how can they afford it?"

She correspondingly lowered her voice, too. "My guess, they're maxing out a new credit card. Earleen has already gone through several—she's told me that."

I nodded sagely and let it go at that.

My cell phone rang as I was paying my check. Ron. We talked as I walked back toward the motel.

"Some interesting news about your guy up there," he said. "First, on the fake identities, I haven't gotten to all of them yet. But one—name on it was David Franklin—there were a couple of contributions to that Social Security account, twenty-three years ago."

"What!"

"Yeah. I noticed that the corresponding driver's license had expired way back, so I ran that one first. The others, if you noticed, were all up to date with current information on them."

I hadn't noticed.

"Looks like David Franklin worked in California for six

months or so and made contributions to Social Security. Can't tell any more than that, and I was lucky to even get that much."

"That's fine." I muddled through this new knowledge as I unlocked the door to the cabin. "What's your take on it?"

"Probably testing the waters," he said. "Got himself a fake ID and wondered whether it would fly. Would he get caught using it. So he gets a job under the fake name, tries it for a few months, figures out that he's okay."

"And his reason for getting this new identity in the first place would be?"

"Who knows? Maybe he'd committed a crime, or planned to commit a crime, wanted a way to get his real name out of the system and start over someplace else. Back then you didn't need identification to buy a plane ticket, but you certainly needed a passport to get out of the country. Could have been something like that in his plans."

"I'll have to do some more digging, see if I can figure out how this ties in," I said. "Meanwhile, I just found out that David's wife and her boyfriend have headed out this morning for Vegas. These people live in a dumpy house and seemingly don't have the extra cash to spend. I want to know how they're doing this trip."

"Breaking news, Charlie, not everyone who goes off to Vegas and blows a bunch of money can actually afford to. I'd bet most of them live in crappy little houses and barely make the rent."

"Okay, you're right. That's true enough. But I'd sure like to know just how much they're spending. It'd give me a good idea about Earleen's position in this whole insurance case up here. I think she thinks she's about to get a huge settlement. So, you want to go to Vegas and check them out?"

"Not hardly. Do you?"

I laughed as I pulled out my keys and let myself into my cabin. "Not hardly. You know how I feel about that place."

"Look, I've got a buddy who owes me a favor. A PI that I

did some legwork for here a few months ago. I may be able to get him to find out something."

"Good enough. I'd just like to know whether they're playing the quarter slots or flashing around big money at the tables."

"Oh, nearly forgot to tell you. I got a call from Continental Union. A guy I knew ages ago works there now and he recognized my name. He opened up a little more than anybody else there has done. Turns out that there wasn't going to be any huge settlement to the family on the Simmons property. Place is mortgaged to the hilt and the mortgage company is breathing down their necks even harder than Earleen Simmons is. Place was in hock for two mil, actually more than its appraised value."

"Wouldn't Earleen know about that?"

"House was in David's name alone, and he alone arranged the mortgage. Funny thing is, the house was once free and clear. When David built it, right after he moved to New Mexico from Silicon Valley, he paid cash. Mortgaged it later. Guess he needed big money for something, but my buddy didn't know what."

"His and Jake's invention, I'll bet." I tried to remember what Jake had told me the cost of the project would run. "They're trying to bring a new medical device to market and I guess the costs are enormous. When did you say this mortgage took effect?"

"Not long before the big boom. January of that same year. The explosion happened in May, right?"

"Yeah."

He hung up, promising again that he'd get his Vegas buddy out to keep an eye on Earleen and Frank.

I caught myself tapping my nails on the desk. Could Earleen have gotten her hands on all or part of that two million dollars? It didn't seem very likely. In fact, I'd just about bet that she didn't know anything about it, not by the way she'd been acting recently.

Maybe I'd underestimated the size of Jake's research project and the impact of their new device being introduced to the market.

It was likely that two million dollars would be a drop in the bucket in that kind of work. I decided that I should ask Jake a few more questions about it.

When I arrived at their house, I found Amanda looking better and seeming a bit brighter than yesterday. She'd been doing dishes and I followed her into the kitchen.

"I guess I have to start getting out, doing a little more," she said. "It's just so hard, until we know for sure about the—" she took a deep breath "—the body. If it's Dad there's a funeral to plan, and I just don't know if I'm up to that yet. The school has been good, though. I'm on paid leave through the end of the term if I want it."

I'd taken a seat at the table while she wiped the counter tops and I just let her talk.

"I'm sure it's him," she said. "I'm bracing myself for that, anyway. I mean, the car's his, the jewelry, the wallet. It's him."

"Twenty-three years ago one of the fake IDs was used. Someone—most likely your father—worked for six months under the name David Franklin. Other than that, we found no activity on any of them. Do you know anything about that? Where he worked, why he might have used another name?"

She stopped cleaning and leaned against the counter. "Twenty-three years ago?" Her face registered absolute confusion. "I would have been seven. I don't know . . ." She struggled to remember. "Second grade. Yeah, I do remember going to a different school in the second grade. We moved from Sacramento to Pasadena. Dad took a new job, but I don't remember anything about it. You know kids, we don't pay attention to much."

I could testify to that. I'd blocked out huge chunks about my parents' lives when I was a teenager, only to have to discover all of it again recently.

"I don't think we lived in Pasadena very long," she said. "We moved to the Silicon Valley after that and Dad did some kind of work in the computer industry. Of course, everyone did.

That's what it was all about out there."

I thanked her for the recollections. They fit with the little we knew, although they didn't exactly answer my questions. We still didn't know why David used another name and made such a quick move and change in careers.

"I really wanted to ask Jake a couple of questions about his work," I told Amanda. "Is he available?"

She almost laughed. "That's really a relative term, isn't it? He's here." The laugh turned harsh. "Available? Jake's not really an 'available' kind of man."

I didn't know what to say to that, but I didn't have to. She turned to the intercom, buzzed the lab and spoke. "Charlie's here and she wants to ask you a couple of questions. Can she come out?"

A fuzzy affirmative came through.

"I have to go to the grocery," she said. "Just go on out there."

At the door, I went through the same procedure of removing my shoes and wearing the paper booties. Jake greeted me from one of the long work tables, busy over some small gadget. He clearly wasn't pleased to be interrupted in the middle of his work day. I got right to the point.

"How much money did David put into all this?" I asked.

He sent me a puzzled look. "Gosh, I think initially it was fifty. Fifty thousand start-up money. Some grant money from back east covered the construction of the building and equipping the lab."

"And was there a big influx later? Say, something around two million?"

"I guess it was about that. Maybe five, six years ago. Just about the time we were really getting the prototype done. Had a lot of legal fees when we began researching and filing all the patent paperwork."

It was more like four years and four months, but I didn't quibble.

"Did David say where that money came from?"

He shrugged. "He might have. Money's not my thing and I don't remember now."

Observing him at the table, shaggy head bent over his work, clearly absorbed in the moment of what he was doing, I could believe it. Amanda's comment about his unavailability seemed to confirm it as well. He looked up at me, questioning, as if to say 'anything else?' and I couldn't really come up with a response. I thanked him, unsure what I'd just learned, except that David really did spend the money here. It wasn't squirreled away somewhere to be hidden from Earleen or to account for a double life somewhere.

Amanda wasn't back from the store yet and I felt like an intruder in the empty house. I left, feeling somewhat at loose ends. Everything seemed to point to David as being the one who'd burned down the house but in that case, who killed him? I wondered, again, whether Earleen and Frank had been involved with each other back then, and perhaps getting David out of the way would then leave Earleen a wealthy widow rather than a divorcee with nothing. Frank very well could have decided it was beneficial to get David out of the picture, if he and Earleen had an inkling about the divorce.

My cell phone rang as I reached the bottom of the hill and I pulled over to take the call.

"Heard from my guy in Vegas," Ron said.

"Already? Wow, he's good. So, he's caught up with them."

"Yeah, you said they were at the Bellagio, right? Well, they no sooner checked in than Earleen Simmons was at the cashier's window exchanging big chunks of money for chips. Ten thousand on the first run, then she went back for another twenty."

"What?" Being one of those Vegas gamblers who allots myself a hundred bucks for a whole weekend, I could not conceive of those kinds of money. "Where'd she get that kind of cash?"

"I wouldn't know about that," he said. "Do we want our

guy to keep watching them? The monetary value of my favor from him is just about used up and it'll start being cash out of our pockets."

I considered it for a moment. "Nah, I doubt anything new will come up. I'm going to check out something else from this end."

There was only one small supermarket in town and it had to be where Amanda'd gone. I spotted Jake's vehicle in the lot and parked beside it. When she came out, five minutes later, with a cart full of groceries I met her at the SUV's back door.

"Charlie!"

"Hey, Amanda. I was hoping I'd catch you. A question came up. Earleen and Frank Quinn have been in Vegas flashing a lot of money around. Any idea where they'd come up with it? I was under the impression they were living on a fairly tight budget."

"A lot? Like hundreds?"

"Like thousands."

Her jaw dropped. A small crease formed between her eyebrows as she thought about it. "When Dad left, disappeared, four years ago, there was probably a few thousand in their joint checking account. It couldn't have lasted long, and I don't think she had access to his bigger accounts, you know, brokerage and such. I assumed the reason she moved in with Frank was to live off him."

"You're pretty friendly with the manager at the bank. You think we might get some information from her?" I asked.

She set the last bag of groceries in the back of the car and closed the hatch. "We can try. Now? I can only spend a few minutes, though. My butter might melt."

The bank was less than a block away and I followed her. Luckily, Susan was free and able to talk to us right away. She gave me a sideways glance but Amanda reassured her.

"All we really need to know is whether Earleen withdrew a large amount from any of my father's accounts in the last few days," Amanda told her.

Susan sat at her computer terminal and was able to bring up the account information simply using David's name.

"Well, it looks like the proceeds from the equity loan, the one we put into their joint checking account on the fifteenth, some of that's been drawn out."

"How much?" I asked.

"Fifty thousand."

"What loan?" Amanda demanded.

"The property on Viejo Road was valued at a hundred fifty thousand. Earleen applied for an equity loan against it, for seventy five thousand. It was approved and the money deposited to the account a week ago," Susan said.

"She borrowed against the land?" Amanda's face had gone white.

"It's legal. Usually on vacant land we can't extend a mortgage for the full value, but she only wanted half. It's prime real estate that would sell quickly if need be."

Amanda turned to me. "But my father was planning to . . ." She realized maybe she shouldn't be quite so forthcoming in front of the banker.

"Thank you for the information," I said.

⊰14⊱

I walked Amanda back out to the cars and asked for directions to the property. It was probably time I took a look at the actual scene of the crime, although I felt pretty sure the police would have removed everything that might resemble a clue in the case.

I followed the main highway through town, made a right turn on County Road D-4 where she'd told me to, and found Viejo Road. It roughly followed the lakeshore, winding closer at times, farther at others, climbing in altitude all the while. I passed one other house, a large chalet-style place with half-timbered walls and stone embellishments. A little farther along stood an elaborate entry to another place, with No Trespassing signs on either side of a heavy wrought iron gate. Amanda had told me to go just past this one, watch the right-hand side of the road, and I'd see a similar gate with 'Simmons' done in tile over the entry. The gate would be unlocked and I could drive in. And so it was.

The drive wound for perhaps two hundred yards and ended at a turn-around. The remains of two stone pillars stood, jagged and weathered, beside it. Beyond those, some charred concrete footings outlined the foundation and a deeper spot where the basement or garage would have been. I could envision the sight of the huge house as one drove up to this spot, to be greeted at the front door by the lord of the manor who would probably have a couple of hunting dogs at his side. The walls would have risen in majestic display, impressing the visitor with Simmons's wealth and prestige. I got out of my Jeep and walked between the two pillars and up a set of flagstone steps that were now covered in a litter of pine needles and a skiff of dirt.

Rusty dashed about, nose to the ground, following what was probably the scent of some rabbit or squirrel. I crossed the threshold, which was about the only thing left of the house itself.

Between the explosion and the fire the gas had done its job in obliterating the structure. Plenty of charred boards lay around, disintegrating now in the aftermath of four years of rain, wind, and snow. Hard evidence, anything that might be considered a clue, had long since been removed. I knew the kitchen stove had been found with the knobs turned to the On positions, and two propane tanks in the garage were also located with the valves open. Those items had surely gone to a lab somewhere for testing, photography, and whatever else the state did to build a case.

Remains of anything valuable—furnishings, a safe, jewelry—were long since gone. As Michaela had told me, the investigators took anything that could lead them to a suspect and Earleen then had the chance to retrieve any of her personal effects that survived. Probably not much. I stood at the spot where the front door would have been but dared not venture farther.

The flooring had burned through in many places and the rest of it was so severely charred that it would be impossible to trust its stability. I could see, through some of the holes, that a crawl space of three or four foot depth lay beneath. I turned away and decided to circle the perimeter instead.

Rusty, by this time, had given up on rabbits and was nonchalantly working his way into the woods. I called to him and he changed course, not raising his nose from the ground.

At the back of the property, the ground dropped away and I could see the appeal of the place, why this particular plot would be worth so much. The forest, which spread out on both sides, opened up here to reveal the lake below. Like a brilliant blue opal in the sunlight, it sparkled up at me, and the mountains beyond—still capped in snow—made the perfect backdrop. An artist could go orgasmic up here.

I could imagine the effect from a second- or third-story deck and allowed myself the fantasy of being up there with Drake, champagne glasses in hand, watching a sunset. I could imagine Earleen wanting this for herself if she'd known David was about to give her the boot. But I couldn't imagine her willfully destroying it. And David? What motive could he have for wanting to tear down something so lovely?

I sat on a flat stone and watched the lake for awhile. The value, clearly, was in the location; the view was spectacular and the sense of peace, high above the lake, pervaded even amidst the burned out ruins. Eventually, Rusty came over and lay down beside me, panting heavily from his run through the forest.

"What do you think, kid?" I asked, scratching his ears. "Who did this? Why did they do it?"

I realized that I'd been looking at everything through present-day reasoning. It was probably time that I went back to the past. The day David left. Everyone subscribed to the idea that he'd simply driven away, but why? Where had he gone and when did he come back, only to end up in the lake?

I tossed a pebble, and it skittered down the hillside, nowhere near the water's edge.

"Let's get out of here," I told Rusty. "I feel like I'm spinning my wheels."

I drove down the mountainside, back to the Horseshoe. I decided to keep the room—I would return and it might be difficult to get accommodations if the popularity of the fishing derby proved true. But right now I thought I might accomplish more back in Albuquerque where I had access to my computer and Ron's expertise in finding out about people's backgrounds. Something about this whole case went a lot deeper than mere jealousy over a woman like Earleen or an argument in a bar. I needed to know what, from David's past, had come back to haunt him.

I phoned Amanda to let her know I was going home for a few days.

"I heard that Earleen and Frank are running through the mortgage money like it was water," she said. "Isn't there something we can do to stop them?"

"I don't know what it would be," I admitted. "She obtained the loan and can spend it as she sees fit."

"Well, a spree in Vegas just isn't right. My father would just d--" Her voice cracked and I could sympathize with her. In her situation, I'd feel the same way.

"I've called Dad's lawyer and am going to meet with him on Monday. We're going to present the new will and see if we can't stop Earleen from getting her hands on anything more."

I wished her luck, although I wasn't sure that Amanda, herself, would get anything until the whole mess was straightened out. Until David's murder was solved everyone would be a suspect.

chapter
⊰15⊱

The drive home was uneventful, but as I neared the city and became swept up in the traffic and noise and glare of headlights I found myself contrasting it with the natural beauty I'd just left up north. I'd lived in a city all my life, had never thought much about it. You know where everything is, you get around, you live your life. But where's the magic? Something about sitting on that mountainside, staring down at that crystal blue lake, had pulled at me with a strange and unknown allure.

The vision burst like a bubble as a pickup truck switched lanes in front of me and I had to hit my brakes. I blew out a breath of frustration as I backed off to give him some space. Maybe Drake and I should talk about this, our lifestyle choices.

By the time I reached the center of town and negotiated the streets toward our office, I'd become thoroughly caught up again in the city experience and the lake in the mountains faded from my thoughts. I turned onto our quiet side street and into the drive of the gray and white Victorian that serves as RJP Investigations' headquarters. Ron's car sat in the parking area behind the house and I pulled in beside it.

Rusty pranced excitedly in the back seat, eager to make the rounds of the yard and find out what he'd missed. Surely some errant squirrel or a neighbor's dog would have trespassed by now. I let him out and went inside while he checked everything.

"Hey," said Ron, "you're back?" He stood at the kitchen sink with a coffee carafe in his hand, looking at it as though he had no clue why the sludge in the bottom was not drinkable.

"It works better if you actually wash the pot at least once a day and make fresh coffee," I said with a nod toward the pot.

"You came back to tell me that?"

I stuck my tongue out at him. There are some brother-sister interactions that will never change, no matter our ages.

"I came back to see what more we might dig up from David Simmons's past." I quickly filled him in on the newest information. "There are all these witnesses who saw him drive out of town that day. No one heard a word from him again, and he turns up dead four years later, less than a mile from home. It's just too weird. And there's the money, lots of money, between the mortgage on the big house, the value of the land, his life insurance."

"Follow the money, I say." He'd set the unwashed coffee pot back on its stand.

I trailed along as he went upstairs to his office, which is just across the hall from mine.

"But right now," he said over his shoulder, "I'm leaving for the day. Going home, cleaning up, and seeing a nice lady for dinner tonight."

"A date?" I stopped in my tracks. Aside from one narrow brush with love, I'd not known my brother to actually go out on a date in years. Not after his nasty divorce from Bernadette.

"Yes, smarty, a date." He plucked his Stetson from the coat

rack in his office, switched off the light, and strode past me while I just stood there with my mouth open.

He was down the stairs and out the back door before the dozens of questions actually had the chance to form in my mind. I damped them back. Not my business.

Rusty came trotting up the hall, apparently getting in as Ron went out. I heard his car start up and drive away.

"Well, that was interesting," I told the dog. "Can you believe it?"

Apparently he had no problem with the news because he went straight into my office and positioned himself in front of the bookcase, pointing directly at the tin of dog biscuits we keep there. I tossed him one of the cookies and sat at my desk. The pile of mail awaiting me looked pretty intimidating. Sally, our part-time receptionist, sorts it each day, giving Ron only the stuff that pertains directly to him. Everything else comes to me because Sally wisely knows that any piece of paper entering Ron's chaotic domain is likely to never see the light of day again. At least she knows I'll handle it and file it correctly including the junk. I began by filing about four pounds of catalogs and advertisements in the circular file. The rest consisted of bills to pay, customer payments to post, and letters to answer—none of which looked appealing at the moment. I stacked them by topic and decided that dinner was in order.

Pedro's Mexican Restaurant has been Ron's and my old standby for years. As I pulled into the tiny parking area, I had the fleeting thought that he might actually bring his date here and I'd get a look at her. But the only vehicles in the lot were Manny's battered pickup and two sedans I didn't recognize.

Pedro greeted Rusty and me with open arms as he called out to Concha that I was here. His rotund little wife is one of those naturally loving people who gathers you up into a squishy hug that's like snuggling into a down pillow. I asked after her sister in El Paso, who'd been ill recently, accounting for Concha's absence on my last two visits. They, of course, inquired as to why I hadn't been in for my customary green chile chicken enchiladas, which led to a quick explanation about my travels up north.

Meanwhile, Rusty settled into the corner beside our usual table and waited patiently for his expected ration of tortilla chips. Manny, the old guy who sits at the bar and downs tequila shooters, raised his grizzly chin in greeting, and the other two couples—tourists, by the look of them—tried hard not to stare at the dog but didn't succeed very well.

"Only one tonight?" Pedro asked, heading toward the bar.

I nodded, wanting to tell him about Ron's date, but knowing the ears of the whole place were already upon us.

Within minutes, I had one of the world's finest margaritas in front of me and Rusty was getting his regular handouts from the basket of chips Concha had set in the middle of the table. I basked in their friendship and wondered what I'd been thinking, pondering a new life in a small town. Look at the fabulous margaritas and enchiladas I'd be giving up.

A half hour later, satiated, I made my way home to find another pile of mail waiting for me. My neighbor, Elsa Higgins, is a jewel—bringing in mail for me anytime I'm out of town, without even being asked. I glanced at her house and noticed she seemed buttoned in for the night with just one light and the flicker of her ancient television set in the living room. I'd call her tomorrow.

I performed the same ritual with the mail here, relieved that about ninety percent of it was trash. By the time I'd emptied my travel bag and thrown a load of dirties into the washer, the letdown began to hit. By nine, I'd showered and settled down with a book but my eyes wouldn't stay open. Tomorrow is another day, I quoted as I switched out the bedside lamp.

The morning dawned with uncharacteristic clouds and dampness in the air. When I opened my eyes I was startled to see that the bedside clock showed 9:43, unheard of for me. The dimness of the room made me want to roll over once more but

I fought it. Today was Friday, perhaps my last chance this week to reach some of the resources I needed to check. After that, I'd probably find myself with two days of empty time. I smiled at that thought and wondered if there were any way on earth that Drake might also have a break and we could hook up somewhere. Rarely does he get to come home during a job, but he gets mandated days off and we sometimes manage quick conjugal visits in a town near the job site.

That idea was quickly shot down a few minutes later. As I dressed in jeans and a light sweater, he called and let me know that they were working through the weekend. His next day off would probably not come for another full week. We made do with some very suggestive conversation and promises of what the next weekend would bring.

I went into the kitchen and fumbled through the meager supply of breakfast options, deciding that the bread would have to be thrown out and none of the cereals were appealing. I would make fresh coffee at the office and see what could be scrounged up there. I gave a quick call to Elsa next door while Rusty gobbled doggy nuggets, then we headed back to the office. The dog settled into the back seat and I, too, soaked in the sights of spring flowers and new leaves on the trees and the peaceful feeling of being back in our familiar routine.

Sally stood at the kitchen sink, scrubbing at the gunky coffee pot, her shaggy blond hair in its usual disarrayed style.

"Doesn't Ron ever wash this thing?" she complained.

"Probably not. And he was a little preoccupied last night." I told her about the date and she was as surprised about it as I'd been. Sally's life is firmly planted around Ross and their little girl, and she's been out of the dating scene way longer than either Ron or I.

"Is he here yet?" I asked.

"Nope, and I was wondering about that."

I didn't want to even think about my brother's getting lucky, especially if this was a first date, so I turned my attention to my office and the mail, which had not magically disappeared during the night. At one point I ventured to stick my head into his office, wondering what he'd done with his notes on our previous David Simmons inquiries, but the desk was way too scary to contemplate. There was no way I'd find a specific bit of information in that mess.

Ron rolled in around noon, looking happy. Not exactly glowing, but chipper. I gave him a quizzical look but didn't ask.

Before he had the chance to get occupied with phone calls, his usual way of spending a big part of the day, I inserted myself into his doorway.

"How much farther back can we go into David Simmons's past?" I asked. I quickly outlined what I knew about the guy's activities near the time he disappeared, and my feeling that there was more to be learned.

"As far as you want," he said in answer to my original question. "Birth certificate, work history, marriage. We could spend months and learn everything there is to know."

"Marriage. Earleen was at least his second, we know, because she's not Amanda's mother. What can we get on that?"

"Depends on where they lived at the time."

"California. Amanda told me she grew up in both Sacramento and Pasadena, then they moved to Silicon Valley—I don't know specifically which town."

"I'll see what I can get." He didn't even complain that he already had too much to do or anything.

"He's got it bad," I told Sally a minute later in the kitchen, as the smell of fresh coffee began to fill the room. "He hasn't grumbled once this morning."

"Yeah, and he's wearing a new shirt. When was the last time Ron bought a new shirt?"

"Wow, I didn't even catch that."

We shushed as we heard his footsteps on the stairs.

"I brought a coffee cake from the bakery," he announced. "Did you see it on the table?"

Sally's eyes widened and I felt mine do the same. My brother is usually the one who comes in demanding that someone else go out for the morning treats. I wanted to meet this lady who'd converted my brother to a gentlemen in such a few short days. When had he met her, anyway?

We helped ourselves to the coffee cake, which had a cinnamon crumble topping that probably contained way too much butter (I refused to check), and went back to our respective duties. Ron gave me a couple of websites to check, while he began a round of phone calls on David Simmons.

Using the data from David's real driver's license from his wallet, we managed to come up with a positive match to a Simmons in Sacramento, where he'd been born on July 21, 1954. The California records tied to a marriage license issued in 1978 to David Simmons and Samantha Bradley. Based on Amanda's age, I could reasonably guess that Samantha was her mother, but I would ask her.

"No divorce decree between those two?" I asked.

"Not yet. If they divorced in another state, it'll take some time to find," Ron said.

Amanda had never mentioned her mother, so I decided to give her a call. Maybe they'd stayed in touch.

"Charlie, my mother died when I was a child," she said, sounding puzzled. "I thought I'd told you that."

I was pretty sure she hadn't but didn't make an issue of it.

"Were you still living in California then?"

"Oh, yes. I was only three. I don't even remember her. It was cancer, I think. Dad just never talked much about it. We were on our own for quite awhile. He met Earleen about the time I left for college."

"And I gather that was pretty much an oil and water relationship, you and her."

"From the start. At first I just felt the kid's normal jealousy over the new woman in my dad's life. Over the years I watched her go through his money and I had the feeling that he felt stuck, that he'd like to get out but didn't know whether he could take the step or not. She manipulated him terribly, everything from the places they'd travel to the television shows they'd watch. She dictated their social life and told him what to wear. The only big battle I ever saw him win was the choice of where to live. She didn't want to come to Watson's Lake. Boy, the fur flew over that one. She wanted to be in L.A. or Vegas. He wanted to be here because Jake and I had moved here the year before. He bought the land and started having house plans drawn up without even telling her. She finally came around when she saw that she'd get the biggest house in town and would have free rein to decorate it as she wanted."

"So why does she stay here now? With him gone for four years?"

I heard a sigh over the line. "I don't know, exactly. I suspect something to do with Frank Quinn. He certainly didn't give her the lifestyle Dad did, but there's something. He's got some kind of hold over her."

I pondered that for a minute. Blackmail of some kind came to mind. But then again, Earleen wasn't the sharpest knife in the drawer. Maybe it was something as simple as a great time in bed with the guy. Maybe they were both biding their time, lying in wait for the insurance settlement, when they'd take the cash and head off for more glamorous places.

Amanda thanked me again for staying on the case and I told her I'd be back to Watson's Lake in a few days.

"Something interesting here," Ron said. I hadn't even heard him cross the hall between our offices. "One of those Social Security numbers you gave me a few days ago? I'd told you he never used it, but that wasn't quite right. He never used it in any employment, so no contributions were made under that name— Mark Franklin."

"Franklin. He used David Franklin as one of the other aliases."

"Franklin was his mother's maiden name, so the logic is there. It was convenient and easy not to get messed up." He held up a hand as I started to open my mouth. "That's not the interesting part. He used the name Mark Franklin to open a bank account here in Albuquerque. I located it at Fidelity State Bank."

I opened my mouth again and got shushed again.

"That's not the truly interesting part," he said. "The account contains nearly four million dollars."

chapter
⇥16⇤

My jaw dropped, I'm sure, and a feeling like a heavy stone settled in my stomach. "Four million?" I managed to croak.

He nodded, as if this kind of news came across his desk every day. "Want to hear more?"

There was more? I could only blink.

"I recognized the address on the account as a mail drop location here in town. Called in a favor to the guy who owns the place."

Thank goodness for Ron's contacts and all the favors people owed him.

"When did you do this?"

"Just now. You were so wrapped up in your online research you didn't even hear me say I was leaving. Anyway, he let me collect the mail from the box and voila—" He held up a stack of envelopes.

I came around the end of my desk and reached for them. "Isn't this completely illegal, us looking at this stuff?"

"Possibly. But we're acting on behalf of David's legal heir. And it's no more illegal than his setting up these accounts under a false identity anyway."

I liked his reasoning. "But—"

"Charlie, just look at what we've got here."

I flipped through the envelopes. Statements from a brokerage house. Two of the envelopes had already been slit open so

I pulled out the contents of the first one. A mutual fund account whose balance topped three million. The second statement showed that another fund contained nearly another four.

I grabbed my letter opener and quickly slit the remaining envelopes open. Most of the statements pertained to the same two accounts. They were merely duplicates of the ones we'd seen.

"Oh my god," I whispered. Over ten million dollars. Where had David come up with this?

I glanced at the postmarks on the envelopes. They'd arrived quarterly over the entire time David had been missing.

"Don't these get sent back to the mailer if they're undeliverable after so many days?" I asked.

"The Post Office does that. But a private mail drop, they don't especially care. They figure they've got a lot of clients who are hiding out in some way. As long as the box doesn't fill to overflowing they pretty much let the customer check their mail as often or as seldom as they want. My buddy didn't remember Mark Franklin, didn't really worry about it 'cause Franklin had prepaid for five years."

"The box didn't contain anything but statements from this one firm, did it? So it looks like David set up this whole identity for only one purpose."

"Kind of looks that way," he said. "Although there were also some IRS notices." He handed me a few more envelopes, which revealed that the government had expected, but never received, tax returns from Mark Franklin.

Something nagged at me. "So, if David had this kind of cash, why did he take out a two million dollar mortgage on the house at the lake?"

"That may be the two million dollar question," Ron said. "Maybe to throw the locals off track, maybe to embellish this little stash . . ." He nodded toward the envelopes.

"No, I don't think that's it." I told him that David had seemingly put the proceeds of the loan toward the invention he and

Jake had been developing. "I know he was successful in Silicon Valley, but this successful? Everyone I've talked to seems to agree that he took his nice profit there and invested in the property and house in the mountains. I don't think any of them have a clue that there was more."

"And I'm wondering about the other identities," Ron said. "We've accounted for two of the four. What else is out there?"

His phone rang just then and he stepped across the hall to answer it.

What else, indeed. David had set up one of the identities and worked under that name, we assumed as a test whether the ruse would work. The second clearly worked as a front for a lot of hidden money. What other uses does someone have for a false name? Skipping the country seemed like a logical reason to me. With a fake passport and access to all this money, David could have disappeared from modern society and be set for life anywhere in the world.

So why didn't he?

When he drove out of Watson's Lake that day, why didn't he head for an airport with ticket in hand and more than twelve dollars in his wallet?

I brooded over it until I began to smell something tomatoey and Italian from the kitchen's microwave. My stomach growled and I noticed for the first time that Rusty had disappeared from his usual spot on the rug near the bay window. Just like him to know when and where food was happening.

Ron was pulling a heated Lean Cuisine dinner from the oven when I got there.

"You're dieting?" I couldn't hide the incredulity from my voice.

He shot me a look.

"Sorry, I mean, hey it's great that you're dieting." I watched him dig through the utensil drawer for a fork and take a seat at the table. "So, are you going to tell me about her? Or is it some kind of State secret."

"I just don't want your opinion about anything," he said.

"When have I ever given my opinion on your love life?"

"The last time."

Okay. But I'd also found out that his little twit girlfriend was deceptive as hell and he was far better off without her.

"I won't do that, I promise. What's her name?"

"Victoria."

Oh shit, the last one was a Vicky. I clamped my mouth shut and nodded. "Where'd you take her last night?"

"Scalo."

Okay, nice place, high class.

"Look, I'm not going to play twenty questions with you," he said. "She's a very nice woman, my age, no kids. Has a decent career and she's not needy, greedy, or seedy. That's all you're getting for now. If things begin to work out for us, I'll introduce you and you'll get all your morbid curiosity satisfied."

I yanked the refrigerator door open with a little more force than I intended, rummaged around until I found an apple, and took it up to my office without another word. I found a blank file folder and jammed all the David Simmons stuff into it, then plopped into my chair and chomped into the apple. By the time I'd chewed until my jaws ached I decided that Ron was almost right. His love life was certainly not my business and he could screw up his life in any way he saw fit. It's just that . . . dammit . . . he's my brother and I don't want to see him hurt again. I blinked away the extra moisture from my eyes, just in time, because his heavy tread sounded on the stairs.

When he peeked around the door frame tentatively, I appeared to be very busy with paperwork.

"Look, I'm sorry," I said. "I'm going to stay completely out of your personal life, okay?"

"Just give me a little time and space. That's all." He went back into his office and I heard him pick up the phone. When the conversation turned sweet, I tuned out.

David Simmons presented more than enough of a puzzle to keep my mind occupied and I resolved to keep to that. I debated calling Amanda again but decided not to. What was I going to say? She clearly knew nothing of this huge stash of his, and bringing it up at the wrong time might cause more harm than good.

I took the brokerage statements back out of the folder and spread them out, studying the dates on the transactions. The local bank account had been in existence for about a year before David's death. No doubt the bank was thrilled that a customer would leave that kind of money in a non-interest bearing account. They'd earned a bundle, no doubt, on what they considered a customer's naiveté.

The brokerage accounts were opened within a few months after that, all on the same day. A huge influx of money had come into David's possession four or five months before he disappeared. No withdrawals, nothing but dividends he'd earned (quite substantial ones), had occurred after the initial deposits. I ran a total on my calculator and found that the number of zeros boggled the mind.

I closed the folder, wondering what to do next. This whole thing was going to get complicated once it became known. Legally, Earleen was still married to David and was now a widow. Under our community property laws she would inherit everything. Unless David had created a trust or something that would leave a portion to Amanda. But we hadn't found any evidence of that yet. The new will could present strong evidence, but it was written as if it would take effect after the divorce. The divorce had not happened, so I had no way of knowing if the will would be deemed legal.

I pictured Earleen and Frank Quinn, squandering money like mad in Vegas, and knew there was no way I could support any plan that would give her tens of millions of dollars while Amanda and Jake struggled day to day. David's letter, the one we'd found at the bank, outlined his wishes but he'd presented so many facets, so many quirks and curves, that I felt uncertain. I wanted to hope that he would want Amanda to have everything.

If Earleen fought it the decision would probably boil down to a court decision and I had a sick feeling that once lawyers became involved the bulk of the estate would filter into their pockets, leaving everyone else out in the cold. I'd seen it happen before.

The other entity with an interest in all this was, of course, the IRS. The brokerage would have reported the dividend income and the government would expect tax returns to be filed. When they got no responses from Mark Franklin, with nothing but a mail drop to identify his location, what would they do? I imagined some sort of attachment on the accounts themselves, but didn't know for sure. I paced to my bay window and stared out at the street below. Two kids from the house across the street played on bicycles. While I watched, their mom called them in for lunch.

"I'm going out for a couple hours," Ron said. He'd donned his Stetson and a suede jacket I'd never seen before.

I put everything back into the folder and jammed it into the back of a file drawer. Officially, Mark Franklin existed nowhere except on these sheets of paper. For now, I intended to leave it that way.

Out the front window I watched Ron's car drive away. Shortly after that, Sally called out that she was also leaving and her minivan left, too.

"So, kid, what do you think?" I said to Rusty. He wagged and looked up hopefully at the cookie canister on the shelf. I unthinkingly tossed him a treat, sat in my chair, got up again. "I'm not focusing too well, am I?" He wagged again but I didn't fall for the cookie ploy this time.

In the kitchen, I toyed with a package of chocolate donuts but tossed them aside. This is ridiculous, I decided. I can't just pace the office all day and think about all that

money. I decided that part of my restlessness stemmed from
the fact that I'd eaten nothing but sugar and coffee all day.
With the generous portions of fried goodies I'd consumed at
Jo's Café during the past week, my jeans were getting snug
and that disgusted me as well.

"Come on, kid," I called to Rusty. "We've got to find
something green for lunch."

I locked up, set the voice mail system, and headed out
the back door. One of the best salad places in town is just a
few blocks away, so I headed there. Virtuously ordering one
with high fiber and low fat, with dressing on the side, I convinced myself that this would be good for dropping at least
a couple of pounds around my middle.

With my salad boxed to go I took it back to the office
and carried it upstairs. The idea of sitting at my desk to eat
seemed, somehow, unsatisfying. I went back down, opened
the front door to the balmy spring air, and sat in one of the
two wicker chairs that have been on the wide front porch
for years, seldom used. It felt good to kick off my shoes and
let the sun hit my feet while I munched at my healthful
lunch.

A couple of birds trilled back and forth at each other, and
the two little boys across the street came back out and took
up their bicycles again. They gave me a long, suspicious
stare, as if they'd never seen a barefoot woman eating a salad
outdoors before. I gave them a little wave and they ducked
their heads shyly.

By the time Ron came back I'd spent all the time I could
justify in the warm spring air and a brainstorm of an idea had
hit me. I logged onto the internet and began searching for
David Simmon's name, looking for anything, past or present,
that might tell me something that neither his family nor his
financial records had thus far provided.

A few newspapers archived old stories in text format, and
I managed to find a couple that actually didn't require a

subscription to get into them. A California paper had carried a story, seven years ago, about the huge dotcom merger of Dyna-Genesis and Syn-Optic, listing David Simmons as the CEO of Dyna-Genesis. I toyed with the words, wondering if the new entity would have been named DynaSynGen or something equally silly sounding. There was one brief quote from David, saying how excited they were to build this dynamic partnership and the usual blurb about how the merger would not affect the status of the two companies' four hundred employees. No photo accompanied the article, but I remembered the company name from something Amanda had told me. It had to be the same David Simmons.

So far, the timing fit with what I knew and logic told me that David himself had netted a nice profit from the merger. But this was more than three years before the huge deposits showed up in the accounts we'd discovered. I kept looking.

Mentions of Dyna-Gen and David Simmons showed up several more times, local California stories that never quite made the national news. Going back in time, I found the notice of the company startup—now twenty years in the past—and the proud announcement that Wells Fargo Bank was financing the new venture, and a short piece that pro-filed David himself. I brought this one up and began reading carefully.

> *Simmons, an MIT graduate and computer whiz kid in the early days of IBM, is venturing out on his own this time with a new idea that he claims will set the comput-er world on its ear. Simmons took questions at a news conference today, but the thing that caught this reporter's attention was the way his nine-year-old daughter, Amanda, stood by his side. Readers may recall that Amanda lost her mother only a few years ago when the family home was tragically destroyed by an explosion*

caused by a gas leak. Simmons barely escaped with the three-year-old Amanda clutched in his arms, but Samantha Simmons died at the scene. Today's announcement . . .

My salad rose in my throat. Two gas explosions in one person's life, two women dying—what were the odds?

chapter

⇥17⇤

The words on the screen floated in dangerously waving patterns as I fought to digest their import. All my ideas about someone trying to get David fell aside at this new information. Had David pulled off a successful insurance scam once before and decided to try it again? Had he succeeded at getting rid of one wife and decided that Earleen's dying would be cheaper than a divorce?

I called out to Ron but got no response. The sounds of clinking glassware drifted up from the kitchen and I waited until I heard his footsteps, upward bound on the stairs. I called his name but couldn't bring my eyes away from the screen, in case the words somehow disappeared.

"Look at this," I said.

He glanced at it, not focusing. "What am I looking for?"

I pointed at the word 'explosion' on the screen. His eyes grew wide.

"Whoa. When was this?"

"When Amanda was about three years old," I said. "She told me her mother died from cancer and she barely remembered her."

"Traumatic shock. An incident like this, she probably wouldn't remember it."

"Exactly. And David made up the other story for her. To protect her, or to hide his involvement?"

"Give me some time on this," he said. "I've got some sources."

While he went back into his office, I continued my internet search, but found nothing older, nothing dating back as far as the explosion that killed Samantha Simmons. I drummed my fingers on the desk, trying to put it all together.

Twenty-some years ago, the Simmons house had exploded, leaving David to raise a young daughter. He moved around a bit, went into business, put together a successful merger. Used the money from that to relocate to the mountains, remarried, built a showplace home, started a new business venture with his son-in-law. Just as this second business is about to make its big breakthrough, he disappears and his new home explodes. Big money appears in his bank accounts but there's no sign of David. Years go by, David turns up dead. So straightforward, yet so complex. My head began to pound.

I could hear Ron's voice on the telephone as I went into the bathroom for some aspirin.

"I got the story, but I don't know how helpful it will be," he said a few minutes later when he came into my office. "A contact at the Sacramento paper went back into the archives for me."

He handed me a fax copy of an old article. A photo showed a dramatic shot of a house completely engulfed in flames. The piece told essentially what we already knew, that only David and Amanda survived the blaze.

"Insurance settlement?" I asked.

"My contact said he thought so. He's looking for a follow up article now, thinks he remembers the paper running more than one piece on the story." The phone rang and he dashed for it.

I heard him mumbling terse responses, which usually means he's taking notes while he listens. He hung up and came back a minute later.

"Got the name of the insurance company. I'll give them a call. The newspaper doesn't know whether they paid the claim or not."

"At least it's helpful to have the name of the company, right?"

"We'll see how much they can tell me. This was a long time ago."

I let him work his magic with the phone while I took Rusty out for a short walk to the backyard. I strode the length of the yard twice at a quick clip, hoping to clear my brain and come up with some answers. I felt better for the brief stretch but still hadn't reached any conclusions.

"Anything?" I said to Ron, noticing he was off the phone when I came upstairs.

"Not much. It's Friday afternoon and some of the office staff have gone home. I reached a mid-level management guy who told me that they normally keep records for seven years. If a claim is paid without dispute the records are destroyed. If the claim was denied or went to court, it may have been kept longer, but he can't say for sure in this case. He's only been with the company ten years. There are other people who've been there longer, but none of them will be in until Monday."

"So what should we do next?"

He shrugged. "What do you hope to accomplish?"

"Amanda hired us to find her father."

"Which has happened. She knows where he is."

"Yes, but there's so much more to it. I think she deserves to know how her mother died, don't you?"

"Will it change anything?"

I felt my teeth clench. "Not materially. But if Continental

Union discovers there was a previous house explosion in David's life, it's going to provide pretty strong reason for them to deny the current claim—as if they don't have reason enough already. That would come as a pretty nasty shock to Amanda if she first learns about it from some suit-and-tie insurance adjuster. I think I better go back up there and meet with her, face to face."

"I agree."

"Plus, if she and Jake don't get the insurance money on the current claim, they're in deep trouble financially."

"I already agreed, Charlie. You don't have to sell me on the idea." He leaned back in his chair. "You going to tell her about those other accounts?"

Over ten million dollars. I hesitated. "Not just yet. I want to see how a few things play out first. They've been secret all these years; another few days isn't going to make a difference."

"I agree on that, too."

"You should have found Victoria sooner. You're being very agreeable today." I grinned and ducked out of the doorway just as a tiny notepad hit the frame.

Back in my office I printed out the article I'd found on the internet and put it into a folder with the other one Ron's buddy had faxed over. Telling Amanda about this wouldn't be easy and I decided that another night at home in my own bed was in order before I made the drive north again.

My neighbor, Elsa, spotted me pulling into my driveway and flagged me down. A guilty twinge hit me as I realized it had been more than two weeks since I'd last spent any time with her.

"Have you had dinner yet?" she asked. Her blue eyes sparkled and the white curls on her head bobbed as she leaned over to pat Rusty.

I thought fast. "I have some pasta and sauce. I could do up a quick dinner for both of us if you can come," I said.

She offered beef stew that she said had been simmering all afternoon. That trumped my jar of Ragu, so I told her I'd be over as soon as I'd fed Rusty. We spent the evening as we used to, with me recounting my day while she listened in the special way that your grandmother has to listen to your childhood tales. As when I was a teen under her care, I left out some of the details and she pretended not to notice. Bless her, she never questioned me too far.

"So you're going back to Watson's Lake in the morning?" she asked, as we cleared the table and ran hot water into the sink.

"Afraid so. Well, with Drake away on his fire contract, I've got to stay busy."

"Would it be okay for Rusty to stay with me?" This was her way of offering me a favor without my having to ask. She'd used the technique on me for years.

"Sure. He'll like that better than trailing around with me in the car all day."

She smiled benevolently at him and I knew he was in for a round of treats that would require several good runs in the park to wear off.

I left her place about nine, cut through the break in the hedge, and arrived home just in time to catch Drake's call. I filled him in on my plans and he told me about the status of the fire. We both hoped we'd get a break by the following weekend and could catch up with each other somewhere.

By eight the next morning I found myself wide awake and antsy to get going. I delivered Rusty and his sack of food into Elsa's loving care and stopped to gas up the Jeep before hitting I-25 northbound. Traffic was light on an early Saturday and I made good time. I threaded my way past a cluster of parked boat trailers, which reminded me of the fishing derby. I was just in time to grab lunch at Jo's; I took the only empty table.

She greeted me like I'd never been gone and filled me in on the latest. Earleen and Frank were back from Vegas. Jo's own opinion was that they'd lost a bundle even though they were talking like typical gamblers, highlighting the big plays and forgetting the overall picture. Amanda was doing all right, but probably wouldn't return to work for a couple more weeks. Rocko Rodman got arrested last night for drunken and disorderly, but what else was new?

I finished my BLT and decided to drop my bag at the Horseshoe Motel before driving out to Amanda's. Selena Gibbons, with all her little bluish curls still perfectly in place, didn't even bother signing me in this time. She handed over the key to my same room and said she still had my credit card number on file. I moved right into the room as if it were my second home.

I debated asking Amanda to meet me somewhere in town, reasoning that bad news is sometimes easier to take when there is other activity going on around you, but on second thought decided that was a bad idea. She'd want to be home where she could absorb the news privately. I got back in the Jeep and drove the familiar roads to their house.

Jake's gray Mazda was parked in the drive and Amanda opened the door before I'd quite reached it, startling me.

"News?" she asked.

"Yeah, let's go inside."

Her bruises from the accident were fading and she moved with a lot less stiffness as she led me into the kitchen. I declined the offer of a sandwich and she put the final touches on one for Jake and walked it out to the lab, giving me a couple of minutes to put my thoughts together.

I did accept a glass of iced tea and she made busy work, looking for sugar and spoons although I had declined both. She kept darting wary glances my way.

"I might as well just come out with it," I finally said. "There really isn't an easy way to tell you this."

She stood at the sink like a statue.

"We came across information about your mother's death and it wasn't cancer. She died in a house fire when you were three. Your father managed to save you, but she didn't make it."

Her mouth worked without making a sound, her lips forming the word 'fire.'

I took a deep breath. "Yes. There was a gas leak. An explosion."

She went completely white and I had to lunge for her tea glass as her fingers went limp. I set the glass on the counter and put an arm around her.

"Come here. Sit." I edged a chair out with my toe and steered her into it.

Her eyes stared widely at a point in space and her lower lip trembled. I knelt in front of her, waiting for the dam to burst. She transported herself back in time, her head waving back and forth, her eyes never leaving that empty spot.

"I don't remember . . ." she said. "I can't . . ."

I patted her hands, which felt like ice. "I know. It's okay. Sometimes we're not supposed to remember the really awful stuff."

"Daddy—we lived in a little white house with big trees in the front yard. I was in the first grade and I walked to school with my friend Marcie from next door."

Obviously, this was several years after the fire, but I let her go on. She needed to work through the process.

"Mama wasn't there. I don't remember her. We didn't have her picture."

How terrible, to lose your mother and all traces of her in one fateful moment. At least I'd always had my home, an attic full of memories about my parents after their plane crash. I tried to rub some warmth into Amanda's hands but they stubbornly remained cold.

Eventually, her zombie-like stare came back into focus and she gave my hand a squeeze.

"I'm sorry," she said. "I don't know why I zoned out like that. I didn't remember her before, why would I remember her now?" She gave a tiny smile. "You can't miss what you never had, right?"

To some extent. But Amanda'd had her mother for three years, three very important years developmentally. I couldn't put myself in her place, exactly, but I knew what she was saying. I backed into one of the other chairs and watched her as she began to run her hands along a paper napkin that must have been left from her lunch. The flat edge of her thumbnail creased the fold into a sharp edge.

"The fire," she said. "There was a gas leak?"

"That's what the news story reported at the time."

"And was my father suspected of setting that one, too?" Her hands became more agitated, grabbing the napkin and ripping little notches in it.

"We don't know. We haven't found anything to suggest that."

She bunched the napkin into a wad and squeezed hard. "Because he didn't do it, you know. He didn't." She stood up and threw the balled paper toward a trash basket in the corner. "My father was a kind and loving man and he didn't cause any fires. I know what people are thinking, that he did it once and then he did it again."

"Amanda, no one even knows about this. No one thinks that."

She whirled on me. "Oh, people in this town most certainly do. They all think he set the gas and drove away. That damned Sheriff Michaela thinks he did it to get rid of Earleen. Not that he shouldn't have, the witch. But he didn't."

"Does the sheriff know about the other fire, when you were little?"

She stopped her pacing. "I don't know. She's never told me."

Obviously. "She probably doesn't know then." I said. "And I'm not going to be the one to bring it up. She's had four years to do her background work on this. She can learn it for herself."

Why I said that, I don't know. Obstruction of justice is not to be taken lightly and I didn't know why I should withhold the information from the law. But, then again, why should I be the one to bring it out? I bit my lip and quashed the thought.

Amanda relaxed visibly. "The two fires can't be related, can they?"

The hope in her voice was so poignant that I couldn't throw a dash of reality at her.

"We're checking a little farther back," I said. "Quietly. No one here is going to learn about our findings."

That seemed to satisfy her and she picked up her iced tea glass again. "I don't even want Jake to know," she said. "It's bad enough that Dad died before they got their product to market. The financial strain has been unbelievable. I hated the fact that the suspicion went toward Dad in the beginning and I really don't want the speculation to start up again."

I nodded.

"You going to be okay?" I asked.

When she assured me that she would, I said goodbye and headed back down toward town. Suddenly the rest of the weekend loomed ahead emptily. I toyed with the idea of driving back to Albuquerque but Ron had already made it clear that we wouldn't learn anything new from the insurance company until Monday. And with Drake away, the house would be too big and too empty.

I cruised the main drag. The two RV parks looked full, and traffic was triple the usual, a lot of it small boats on trailers. A man was washing the windows of a gift shop and another place was getting a fresh coat of paint. I realized that the summer season would soon be upon us and this little town, so dependent on tourism and the allure of the lake, wanted to put on its best face. At the tiny bookshop on the corner, I stopped and browsed, having finished the Slater mystery and wanting to find something equally good to occupy my mind. I came away with two paperbacks and a small box of chocolates.

Back in the cabin, I snuggled into the comfy easy chair in the corner after brewing a cup of tea with my travel coil. The chocolates somehow dwindled and I got up once, just to switch on a light. David Simmons, insurance claims, and ten million cash fell away into obscurity as I lost myself on the moors of England.

chapter
ᢒ18 ᢒ

Sometime around one in the morning I finished the first book and turned out the lights. It was nearly noon when I opened my eyes, realizing that I'd not been awakened by a wet nose on my arm nor, unfortunately, by a warm body beside me. I stretched and missed each of them briefly, wondering what Drake was doing right now. Although my habit at home is to get up and start the day early, I felt no compunction toward that today. The covers were warm and I was perfectly happy to stay there.

Eventually, though, life intruded. I heard car doors slamming outside as a few other guests packed up and got ready for the Sunday drive back to wherever home might be. I finally got up, showered, and dressed in loose sweats and a T-shirt. The second paperback called out to me but I knew it would be very easy to simply plop back in that chair and do nothing for another whole day. I picked up my key and walked to Jo's.

The place was filled with cheerful customers, enjoying their weekend breakfasts and lunches out, and I ordered and ate quickly to make room for other newcomers. Before settling in to read, I decided I really should get some exercise so I left Jo's and headed toward the lake. A walk along the shore, fresh air in my face, would do me good.

I set a brisk pace and put in a couple of miles before the altitude began to make me puff a bit. Slowing as I neared the marina on my way back, I saw Earleen Simmons talking to a man beside a white pickup truck. Their voices carried on the clear air, rising and dropping so that the words didn't come through clearly. But the tone did. I caught a couple of expletives, then the man got into the truck, slammed the door and spun out in a cloud of dust.

Earleen stood with her fists on her hips and watched him go. When she whirled toward her own car, she caught sight of me watching her.

"What?" she demanded.

I shrugged. "Nothing. Nothing at all. Just wondered if you were in trouble there."

"Well, I'm not. I'm just goddamn peachy."

I stepped a little closer. "You don't sound peachy, Earleen. Want to tell me about it?"

"No." She reached for her door latch and paused. "What are you still doing hanging around here? Is Amanda wasting money again, having you poke around into things that aren't your business? Wish I still had that kind of cash."

I almost blabbed that Amanda didn't really have money to spare, but held myself back.

"That damned girl and her father. Never saw people who could run through money the way they did." Coming on the heels of her recent trip to Vegas, I found this laughable, and it must have showed on my face.

"Hey, don't you dare give me that," she said, leaving the car and advancing on me, index finger extended. "I had a fine life before I met David Simmons. Now what have I got? Diddly-nothing."

"Sorry, I didn't realize that."

"Yeah, well. There's lots you don't realize," she mocked. "I did good for myself, back in California. I met David, I lived in a nice house, had a car that beat this piece of shit all to hell, and a great job. We move out here, he's all into this invention, and my money's all used up before I know it."

The anger welled into tears of frustration and she turned to face away from me and brush at them.

"Earleen, I'm sorry. I thought David made a fortune in the Dyna-Gen merger."

"Oh, he did. Then he decides to follow precious little Amanda out here to the sticks and foolish me, I come with him. At least I had a beautiful home here." She sniffed loudly. "And now I don't even have that."

She stomped back to her car, then wheeled on me again. "And for your information, that guy—" she waved vaguely in the direction the white pickup had gone—"that guy is somebody who cares. He's helping me start a new business."

The lie was so blatant I didn't bother to respond.

"You got a mortgage on the land. Why didn't you consider selling the land and building yourself a nice little place somewhere else?"

She looked at me like I'd come from another planet. "You wouldn't understand."

Oh, I thought I did. I watched her start the car and drive away. Frank Quinn seemed to be the number one reason. Why women hook up with losers like that, then feel that they have no options—it's beyond me. I felt no sympathy for someone who squandered away borrowed money in Vegas, then complained about having nothing. Earleen had plenty of options but she'd closed herself off to most of them.

I traced my way from the marina to the highway and fast-walked along it until it became Main Street. Back in my cabin I drank two full glasses of water and was about to succumb to the allure of my book when I noticed a message light blinking on the phone.

Ron's voice came through, telling me he was putting in a few hours at the office and had some new information. On a Sunday?

Once again I wondered why he hadn't simply called my cell phone, then I realized I hadn't taken it with me. Sure enough, he'd left a nearly identical narration there. I dialed the office and waited four long rings before a strange female voice answered, "RJP Investigations."

"Who is this?" I demanded.

"Victoria Baker. Who's calling please?"

Victoria. The voice was pleasant and businesslike but the fact that she was in my offices, answering my phones, irked.

"This is Charlie Parker, one of the owners of the office you're standing in. Please put Ron on the phone."

"Oh, Charlie. It's wonderful to talk with you," she said. "Ron's told me so much about you."

That irked even more, since he told me nearly nothing about her.

"I'm really looking forward to meeting you when you get back to town," she said.

I bit back the irritation and made my voice neutral. "Ron left a message for me, some new information on our current case?"

"Oh, yes. One moment." She put me on hold.

"What is she doing answering our business lines?" I demanded when Ron picked up.

"Charlie, don't go there." His voice came through low and firm, partially muted as if he were cupping his hand around the mouthpiece. "I was on the other line and asked her to answer. I knew you'd be calling."

I wanted to snap out some retort about it being unprofessional to have a girlfriend answering the phone, but I bit it back. She'd handled it very professionally and anyone but myself would have assumed her to be our regular receptionist. I took a deep breath and resolved to drop it.

"Okay. You said you have some new information?"

"Just an interesting tidbit. I'll know more tomorrow when I reach the insurance company from the first Simmons fire. Just thought you'd be interested to know a little background on Samantha Simmons. Samantha Bradley Simmons."

Nothing clicked.

"Bradley. Of Bradley Electronics. Founder of the chain store of everything electronic, the chain that's now got a branch in every American city and a good number of them in Europe, too."

"The Big Brad chain?"

"Exactly. Big Brad Bradley was Samantha's grandfather. Back in the fifties he latched onto the potential of television and started a store that sold only TV sets. Carried a few radios as a sideline, and eventually branched into stereo equipment. By the sixties he had forty stores across the country, and was probably adding computers around the time Samantha was born, well before anyone else in the country thought the new gadget would ever take off."

"And David, knowing the Bradley reputation, latched onto the prestige of the family name?"

"And the money. When Samantha turned twenty-one she inherited a big chunk of cash and a twenty percent interest in the company. David married her three months after her twenty-first birthday."

"And stayed in favor with Big Brad?"

"Samantha's grandfather died around that time—heart attack. He was a guy who loved his big steak dinner and whiskey. Her father, Brad Junior—no one ever had the nerve to call him Little Brad—was running things by then. Other siblings and their offspring also served on the Board of Directors, and it was a tightly held family business."

"Did Samantha participate? Draw a salary, that sort of thing?"

"She apparently got her stock dividends, but she'd moved off with David to pursue his career. She had Amanda and became a full-time mom during those years."

"Then she died in the house fire."

"Yes. David kept Amanda to himself, out in California. The rest of the family in Illinois didn't have contact with her. When Samantha died, her stock reverted back to the core family and the shares were divided among her cousins. David got none of it. He raised a stink for awhile but wasn't able to break the iron-clad rules of inheritance that the Bradley clan lives by."

"You mentioned a chunk of cash that Samantha received on her twenty-first birthday."

"A million dollars. Yeah, well it didn't last long. Being young and frivolous, Samantha and David went through it pretty quickly. Bought a big house, two fancy cars, and a boat. It's the same house that she died in a few years later, and they'd had it under-insured, so David came away without a whole lot to show for his years on the fringes of the Bradley family."

"That must have made him bitter," I said.

"Might have. He seemed, though, to settle into a simpler lifestyle, raising his daughter and working hard."

I mulled it over after we hung up. Seemed way more than coincidence that a man would marry twice, lose two homes to gas leaks, and come out with several fat bank accounts that no one knew about. I just couldn't see how either Samantha's money or Earleen's humble assets translated into the staggering amounts in those accounts now. He'd never had access to more than a million dollars at once, and it was pretty obvious where that had gone.

Amanda had never mentioned the Bradleys nor did it seem she had inherited any of their money. She and Jake wouldn't be in their current financial pickle if that were the case. Unless she had her mother's lack of judgment and had allowed Jake to use up her money on his invention. I pondered that while I paced the cabin.

Settling down with my book and spending Sunday lazily doing nothing sounded like a good plan but I couldn't seem to focus. David Simmons: the more I knew about him, the more of a puzzle he became. Money seemed to be an obsession with him, but to talk to Amanda, she only remembered the fun times they shared and the fact that he'd been a good father. He'd accumulated a fortune but kept it secret. He'd set up false identities but used them only in limited ways. His entire life seemed full of lies and deceptions. I wondered how much Amanda knew about the Bradleys.

I dialed her number but got no answer. Undoubtedly, if Jake were out in his lab he didn't interrupt work for the telephone. If Amanda wasn't home, she was probably somewhere in town, and that was easy enough to find out.

Basic detective work 101 includes lots of surveillance and routine legwork. I started my Jeep and began at the east end of town. Beyond the Horseshoe Motel stood a couple of others and a drive-in taco place. I cruised them and didn't spot the Zellinger vehicle. Along Main Street, I scanned the smattering of cars around the church, the few businesses that were open, and the park. Jo's Café and the ice cream parlor held, by far, the largest number of patrons but I didn't spot the gray Mazda at either of them. By the time I got to the west end of town, noting that the post office parking lot was empty and the gas station next to it had just one car with Colorado plates, I decided I must have missed her. I pulled over to the shoulder to figure out my next move, and the Mazda buzzed past me, coming from the direction of the marina.

I pulled in behind Amanda and followed her to the bookstore.

"Finished those other two books already?" The owner greeted me with his usual friendly smile.

"Uh, almost." I glanced around and saw Amanda at the magazine rack.

"Hi." Now that I had her within reach, I became a little uncertain about how to start the conversation. The guy behind the counter clearly had nothing else to do but eavesdrop on our conversation and I wasn't about to give him fodder for the latest bit of juicy town gossip. I browsed the history section until Amanda made her choices and chatted with the man at the counter. When she walked out the door, I quickly caught up.

"Amanda. Got a minute?"

She smiled. "I figured it wasn't mere coincidence that you happened into the bookstore at the same moment I did. What's up?"

We moved into the shade of a huge elm tree, appearing to the rest of the world like two women chatting about their newest recipes.

"Are you close at all to any of your mother's people?" I asked. "The Bradleys?"

She shook her head. "I haven't even heard that name in years. I suppose somewhere in the past my dad must have mentioned them. I know the name, that's about all."

"It never came out that they're the Bradleys of the Big Brad electronics chain?"

Her eyes went wide.

"I take it that's a 'no.' "

"The Big Brad chain? I don't think that's possible, Charlie."

"Our investigation brought it up. Your mother, Samantha Bradley, split off from them when she married your dad. We're not sure why. Just wondered if he'd ever said anything about that."

"Not a word." A small crease etched her forehead. "I can ask Jake if Dad ever mentioned it to him."

"Would you mind if I came along? We could ask him now. If you were on your way home, that is."

She glanced around. "Well, I am. Sure. Is your . . ." She spotted my Jeep. "Want to follow me up there?"

Jake was, as usual, busy in the lab when we arrived. He seemed grumpy as he put down a slide he was working on under the microscope and removed his face mask. Amanda and I waited at the doorway, well out of the work area, until he joined us. I repeated what I'd asked Amanda about the Bradley family.

Jake gave it a moment, seeming to concentrate on remembering something. "I don't think so," he finally said. "We didn't talk much about the past. David was the kind of guy who was very much in the moment. Whatever the current project, that's where his attention stayed."

Amanda nodded. "Absolutely. If we were at the zoo, when I was a kid, he'd be just as focused on that bear or seal as any kid in the place. When he was building the house here, he gave his whole attention to the details. Same with Jake, here in the lab. The two of them could work in here for hours."

"Okay, thanks," I said. "I wondered because Samantha got quite a large inheritance from the Bradleys. If David had stayed in touch with them, they could have been a good source for cash in your work here, Jake."

A shadow passed across his face but he didn't say anything.

Amanda's chilly hand on my arm got my attention. "A large inheritance? When did that happen?"

"At her twenty-first birthday. Right before she married your father. Our reports show that they bought several high-dollar items, so it's doubtful there was much left by the time you were born."

She pressed her fingertips to her temples. "I . . . there's something about that . . . some money. My mother and dad arguing." She squeezed her eyes shut, remembering. "I don't know. I can't come up with the specific details. I must have been two or three. Can kids have memories as young as two? I don't know. It's just an impression of a big fight. She yelled something about money, about what it would cost him if she died."

Her face had gone pale and clammy-looking.

"I just don't remember."

chapter
⇥19⇤

I thought about Jake's comment about David's proclivity toward living in the moment as I drove down the mountain, toward the Horseshoe. Again, more complexities. If David truly lived in the moment, spending money as quickly as it passed through his hands, how did he manage to hide away ten million dollars in accounts no one knew about? How did the fake IDs fit? The planning that went into that had to be enormous. And he surely had some plan for the use of the other identities; one doesn't set up multiple lives unless one has a reason to do so. But damned if I knew what those reasons were. Some vital bit of the puzzle was still missing.

The rest of the afternoon slid by as I read the words in my new paperback without absorbing them. By five o'clock I gave up on that, had a sandwich at Jo's, followed by a walk through town in the last of the daylight.

I dreamed fitfully in disjointed scenes where I was alternately home with Drake and then in Jake's lab here in the mountains. David Simmons came into some of the scenes and when he spoke it was with a high, reedy voice that seemed completely unfitting with the six-foot, burly build of the man. The huge house by the lake was intact and I walked through the rooms with Amanda, until Ron showed up unexpectedly to tell me that I needed to find a safe in the study and look in it. I woke up more tired than I'd been when I went to bed the night before. The clock said 5:21. I groaned and rolled over. There was really no point in trying to go back to sleep.

I splashed water on my face and brushed my teeth, ran a brush through my hair and pulled it up into a ponytail. Wearing gray sweats that matched the circles under my eyes, I stepped out to the porch and took in a few lungfuls of mountain air. I made myself bend to touch my toes three times and did a quick little jog in place. A good cup of coffee would get me on the way to actually being awake.

The town seemed curiously silent after the bustle of the weekend. I walked up to Jo's, waving at Woody as he arrived at the Chevron across the street. The locals had begun to recognize me, minus the curious stares, and I briefly envisioned what it would be like to simply stay here and fit into their little society. It might not be all bad. I pictured the land where the Simmons house had stood, with its majestic views and peaceful solitude. How much would it take to buy that plot?

I shook off the thought. Don't be dumb, Charlie. You've got a business to run in Albuquerque and Drake's got huge commitments with the helicopter service. You can't be moving off to paradise. Pair-o-dice was more like it. Making a living in a little lakeside village would be a big gamble. It always is, in resort towns.

Four vehicles sat outside Jo's and they turned out to be a construction crew who occupied one table, boisterous men enjoying a hearty breakfast before heading out for their day's work. I took a seat at the counter and Jo filled a mug for me without asking. I let the hot brew course through my veins before picking up the menu. The construction guys left and a few others drifted in, including two couples and a woman with two young children.

"So, you going to the Simmons memorial today?" Jo asked as she poured my third refill.

I felt a stab of irritation that Amanda hadn't said anything about it to me. If Jo knew, then everyone at the café knew. Why didn't I? Maybe I wasn't fitting in with the locals as well as I'd thought. I shrugged it off, telling Jo I probably would go. I finished my French toast in a grumpy mood.

When I got back to the cabin, the message light on my phone was blinking. Amanda, letting me know of the service and pleading with me to come, apologizing that she'd forgotten to mention it yesterday but the plans were made on short notice, yada, yada. I called her back to let her know I'd be there.

"I'm so sorry, Charlie. I should have told you that the sheriff released the body. Somehow, the state lab got right on it and made the positive ID." Her voice went quavery.

"It's okay. Our other conversation got a little intense. Are you doing okay?"

She assured me she was, although when she reiterated the invitation to the service a little desperation crept into her voice.

The service would be at ten, so I had hours yet. I used my fresh caffeine-and-sugar fix to go for a long walk, circling by the elementary school and down the block past the house Earleen and Frank shared. I crossed the main road and strolled by Billy Rodman's place, which looked belted up and quiet. The brothers were supposedly off in county jail and I wondered how long that would last. I couldn't imagine that drunken and disorderly carried a very huge penalty, considering a bunch of our state legislators did it all the time.

By nine forty I'd had time to shower and rummage through my small stash of clothing for something appropriate to wear and had driven to the chapel of the little multi-denominational church that served the community. I hate funerals and usually refuse to go—too many memories from my own youth. But Amanda had practically begged and I got the feeling it was because she and Jake would be sitting across the aisle from

Earleen and Frank. She must have wanted to beef up her rein-
forcements just a tad. I found her among the small crowd in the
lobby—including the mayor and sheriff and a group of churchy
looking ladies I'd never seen before.

Amanda squeezed my hand and leaned in to whisper.
"Thanks for coming, Charlie. I can use the moral support."

Sure enough, Earleen stood across the room, barely con-
cealing the daggers in her eyes.

Amanda took Jake's arm—somehow he looked even
younger in a suit than in his lab coat—and I followed them into
the chapel. A deacon directed us to take the front row on the
left side of the aisle, and almost immediately Earleen and Frank
took the same row on the right side. Amanda, I noticed, busied
herself with a handful of tissues.

The interminable business of doleful music followed by
someone—the minister, I assumed—waxing eloquent about all
of David's wonderful qualities began. I half-listened, not catch-
ing anything new, any bit of information that would let me
know what had happened to him. No one jumped up and
admitted to being the one who'd bashed him over the head, and
being in the front row I couldn't even sneak a peek backward
to see if any uncomfortable fidgeting was going on back there.
I assumed that would be Michaela's reason for being here.

We endured thirty minutes or so of comforting words—at
least I assumed Amanda found them comforting to some
degree. What do you say to the family when someone's been
murdered? And there's not much at all you can say when the
dead guy is also suspected of killing someone else.

When we stood up to let the mourners file past, I stepped
aside and watched. Aside from family, there were only about
twenty people there and most of them just glanced furtively at
the closed casket before offering tentative handshakes to the
Amanda team and the Earleen team. It was almost humorous to
watch, but I wasn't there for the fun of it. The chief suspect was
inside the casket, the secondary one was in county jail, and the

rest of them stood in the receiving line. I studied the faces but saw nothing out of the ordinary at all.

Burial would take place at the community cemetery about ten miles away. A hearse bore the casket but everyone else was on their own in private cars. Once I ascertained that Amanda and Earleen would not somehow be thrown together in one vehicle I whispered to Amanda that I'd take my own.

"You'll come with us to Horton's office afterward, won't you?" she said. "He'll be reading the will."

Now that could get interesting.

I followed, noting that the crowd had dropped off by at least half, leaving only the immediate family, the sheriff, Horton Blythe, and a few others to actually stand at the graveside. That part of it went quickly. There wasn't a whole lot that hadn't been said at the church. I stifled a yawn.

Two of the churchy ladies told Amanda that they'd bring food by her house. She thanked them, although I could tell she really didn't want any company. She told them she wouldn't be back at home for another couple of hours and they exchanged satisfied smiles. I could envision casseroles and cakes going into ovens, to be produced hot and fresh at the right moment. Amanda sent me a "Help me" look, so I engaged the two women in one of those meaningless conversations about how well they knew David. I let them natter on until I noticed people getting into cars. At that point I exited with a line that bordered on rude, I'm sure, but it was more important that I follow the Zellinger's car to Blythe's office.

We made a cozy little procession—Horton Blythe in a champagne colored Cadillac that couldn't have been more than two years old, Earleen and Frank in Frank's swashy Olds sedan that had to be twenty years out of date, Jake and Amanda in their gray SUV, and me in my Jeep. I wondered at the conversations that must be taking place in the other vehicles. A fly on the windshield could get some juicy tidbits, I felt sure. Too bad I hadn't thought to install tiny recorders.

We headed out the cemetery gates, in the opposite direction of Watson's Lake, and followed the winding two-lane through the mountains toward Segundo. The town of around 5,000 inhabitants, which serves as the county seat, is about thirty minutes from Watson's Lake and it was bustling with noonday traffic when we arrived. If I'd given much thought to where people of the region could go for junk food and major shopping (we're talking one small Wal-Mart store), I'd just found the answer. A KFC, a Taco Bell and a McDonald's represented the fast food contingent, and all three had cars queuing up to their drive-throughs like ants toward a sugar cube.

Blythe's office was one block off the main street in a territorial-style building that blended perfectly with the architecture of the whole town. Even the McDonald's, I'd noted, was adobe-colored with vigas. The law offices occupied half the building, while a title company and a mortgage firm filled two smaller slots. With almost military precision, we filed into the lot. It became interesting to watch the way people chose their parking spots. Horton, in the lead, took a reserved spot with his name on it, inside a fenced area at the back of the building. Frank almost followed but hit the brakes when he realized what a social faux pas that would be. Everyone else consequently had to hit the brakes, too, and this resulted in a moment of indecision. My tail end was sticking out into the street so I mentally urged them on. Frank ended up taking the only spot he could maneuver the huge Olds into, and I watched Amanda direct Jake to take the first empty space near the door. I pulled in next to their Mazda, a small buffer in case the Olds should become belligerent later on.

We stood beside our respective vehicles, shuffling uncertainly, until Horton Blythe bustled forward and ushered us toward the front door.

"Come in, come in," he said, almost impatiently. "My secretary should be—ah, yes. Cathy, coffee in the conference room, please."

The forty-something woman in navy pinstripes rose and disappeared into a side room.

The rest of us followed Horton through a set of double doors and into a long room with a conference table set for six. Cathy had somehow circumvented the congestion in the hallway and appeared now through another doorway, tray and full coffee setup in hand. She quietly offered the beverage around as we all took seats—Horton at the head of the table, Earleen and Frank to his right, Amanda and Jake to his left, which left me at the foot. I felt a little strange being here, but certainly had as much right as did Frank Quinn, so I wasn't going to apologize for my presence. Frank was the only one to accept the offer of coffee and Cathy left the tray on a sideboard and quietly exited. Horton had pulled a leather portfolio from somewhere and now began to extract a sheaf of papers.

"We are gathered for the reading of the last will and testament of David Simmons," he began and I tuned out the rest of the formal introduction as he went through some extraneous introductions of the parties in the room. Since everyone knew everyone else, I could only assume the formality was something Blythe performed as routine.

I sat back to watch the reactions. It didn't take long. I knew Amanda had already talked to Blythe about the will we'd found in the safe deposit box, but I wasn't sure whether Earleen knew about it. My suspicions were confirmed about a minute later when Horton finished the lawyerly sounding bits and began speaking as David's long-time confidant.

"David Simmons drew up a new will approximately two months before his disappearance," Blythe said. "In this document he made provisions for some life changes he expected to happen shortly thereafter."

I could tell by the blank look on Earleen's face that she had no clue what was coming.

"To my wife Earleen, a copy of the prenuptial agreement she signed, agreeing to leave the marriage with nothing, and a copy of the divorce papers which I plan to file on this date." When Blythe actually read the words, cutting Earleen out entirely, her face went white and her mouth hung slack. I almost felt sorry for her.

Frank's expression looked like someone who'd just swallowed strychnine. His eyes bulged slightly and he began to sputter.

"Mr. Quinn, there will be no comment." Blythe looked up briefly and returned to the papers in front of him.

"To my daughter, Amanda Zellinger, my home and property at Watson's Lake, New Mexico, my personal effects, and all monetary and brokerage accounts in my name."

I stifled the cough that threatened to close off my throat. In my name. So, what had been David's intentions toward all the money he'd stashed under other names? I glanced toward Amanda, but remembered that she knew nothing about the rest of the money.

Earleen recovered her powers of speech and lit into Blythe. "That's ridiculous and completely unfair. We weren't divorced yet."

Horton Blythe ran his manicured nails over the document. "His wishes were plain. And you did sign the prenuptial—"

"Those things never stand up in court," she yelled. "I'll fight this."

He met her eyes coolly. "If you have the resources, you have that privilege."

"You've signed a mortgage for fifty-thousand dollars on my property," Amanda reminded her. She turned to the lawyer. "Since she arranged that mortgage after my father's death, and since this will would have been in effect at that time, isn't she legally bound to repay the money to me immediately?"

"I think you're right, Amanda," he answered. "In fact, there could be criminal implications—I'd have to research that part of it."

Frank clenched his fists and gave the lawyer a deadly stare.

"You little bitch!" Earleen screamed. "You talked him into this. You never liked me!" A rim of white foam began to form at the corners of her mouth.

Amanda pulled back into her chair, tucking herself as far from her screaming stepmother as she could.

Horton Blythe rose and faced Earleen squarely. "Do I need to summon the police?"

She took a step back but didn't lose a scrap of her anger. "It won't do any good. I'm not sitting still for this."

Frank reached out to take her arm but she shook herself away from him. She strode past him and shot one backward glare at the room. "You'll be hearing from my lawyer." The electricity in her voice left a silent vacuum as she jerked the door open and stalked out, Frank stomping along behind.

We heard the front door slam, giving a shudder to the building, and Horton stepped to the windows that faced the parking lot. We could hear the rumble of the shabby Olds as Frank started it and it roared out of the driveway. As the sound retreated, I let out a pent-up breath.

"Well, it went about as I expected," Amanda said. The rest of us dissipated the tension with nervous giggles. "Can she really contest the will?" she asked.

"There's a clause specifically writing out anyone who contests it," Horton said. "But that doesn't mean she won't try. She's got nothing to lose, obviously."

"I'm willing to let her off the hook for the fifty thousand," Amanda said, "if she'll leave town and drop all intentions of pursing this. Can you write up something legal-sounding to that effect?"

Blythe agreed and they sat down to sketch out some details.

The murderous look on Frank Quinn's face stayed with me. Nothing to lose and everything to gain. I wondered about the will's provisions if something happened to Amanda.

⊰20⊱

I followed Jake and Amanda's vehicle back to Watson's Lake, watchful at every driveway and side road for the powder-blue Olds. Amanda might think she could rid herself of the threat by throwing Earleen a bone, but I wasn't so sure. Earleen was self-centered and spiteful, but Frank Quinn seemed dangerous. He'd hooked up with the rich widow for a reason and he didn't seem the type to simply blow it off. I debated it for the whole drive; Frank clearly wasn't ambitious enough to make a fortune on his own, but he might go to great lengths to get one dishonestly. It made me glad I'd not mentioned the really big money to anyone yet.

It was after two o'clock when we hit the outskirts of Watson's Lake. Amanda and Jake turned off the highway at Piedra Vista, heading toward their house. I'd told her I would come up there, but first I wanted to see if I could get a handle on what Earleen and Frank might have in mind. It was only slightly out of the way to cruise the main drag, and sure enough, I spotted the Olds at the Owl Bar. Adding alcohol to their tempers might be like gasoline on a fire, so it seemed prudent for me to let the sheriff know what had transpired.

I found Michaela in her office and briefed her quickly on the lawyer's revelations. She assured me that a deputy would be on the streets.

"I've got the feeling those two will drink a little too much and may need to sleep it off in custody tonight," she said with a wink.

I left, unsure whether I'd really conveyed the danger, but knowing I'd done what I could for the moment. At the Zellinger place, I found the mood subdued, the natural result of the emotional morning.

"We've got food, if anyone's interested," Jake said. "The ladies brought chicken casserole, green bean casserole, Jell-O salad, and a pineapple upside down cake. Want me to reheat the casseroles?"

Amanda waved away the notion of food, and while I can usually go for anything at any time, I wasn't all that hungry either. Jake made up a plate and nuked the hot foods for a minute.

"Come on, sweetie, you need to eat." He placed the plate on her lap and handed her a fork. "You hardly had anything yesterday, either."

I had to give him points in the solicitous department. I'd never seen him act quite so caringly toward his wife, even after her car accident. She sent a weak smile his way and poked at the chicken with her fork.

He gave me an inquisitive look and I agreed to also take a plate. The three of us sat in the living room with plates on laps, wondering what next. Conversation meandered among inconsequential subjects, carefully staying away from David or Earleen. I had already told them, when I arrived, about my stop to Michaela's office.

Jake cleared the plates and I heard him in the kitchen, washing up. I called out an offer to help, but he assured me he could handle it.

"This is so rare, I'm not going to say a word," Amanda told me in a low voice. "I wasn't even sure he knew where the plates were kept until today. I mean, this is a guy who grabs himself a sandwich and eats it off a paper towel. Doing for anyone else, well, that just doesn't happen."

She glanced toward the kitchen door. "Things have been strained between us for a long time. Between money worries and the uncertainty about Dad, well, I just haven't been sure we'd make it."

I came close to mentioning the other bank accounts then, but something held me back.

"We'll see," she said.

Jake came back into the living room, this time bearing a tray with squares of the cake on plates and a carafe of coffee.

"I'm impressed," I said. "You're pretty handy with this stuff."

Amanda didn't say anything but she kissed his cheek when he handed her a plate. He polished off his cake quickly and looked surreptitiously at his watch.

"Go, go," she finally said. He gave her a sweet smile and yanked at his tie. Moments later he emerged from the bedroom in casual clothing, heading for the lab.

"He never can seem to settle down in a social situation. That lab is everything."

"I don't want to spoil the mood, and I don't want to be just another workaholic," I said, "but I feel like there are still unanswered questions. You hired me to find your father, Amanda, and that didn't turn out as anyone hoped." Anyone but Earleen. But then she'd also had her major disappointments this week. "I'm wondering how much longer you want me to stay on. The police are handling the murder investigation."

She set down her cup and ran her fingers through her hair. I noticed that the creases beside her mouth had become more pronounced in the past week.

"I can't help but feel that Dad's death is going to go unsolved," she said. "The initial investigation was so intent on the idea that he set up the gas leak that they didn't really investigate any evidence that pointed to anyone else."

"Do you know what evidence? What other suspects?"

"Well, not directly." She sighed. "Not really. I just know he didn't do it, and now that he's dead, doesn't it seem logical that someone, whoever killed him, probably did it because they'd also set the fire and he could have identified them?"

I had to agree with the logic.

"I'd like you to keep looking into it, if that's what you're asking."

"How long has Frank Quinn been in the picture with Earleen?" I asked.

"I don't know, exactly. Longer than he should have been, I suspect." She picked up her cup again and found the coffee had gone cold. When she came back from microwaving it, she said, "I'd finished my student teaching, driving to Segundo every day because there were no positions open here at the time. So I wasn't around Dad and Earleen a whole lot during the three or four years before the fire. By the time a job came up here in town I was so happy to get it that I really devoted all my spare time to impressing the principal and my students and their parents.

"Dad had moved here a year after Jake and I did. We were always close, Dad and I, because of Mom . . ." She got a far-away look but went back on topic. "Anyway, we kept talking about how much we loved the lifestyle in the mountains and Dad thought that sounded appealing, so he wanted to come here, too. He and Earleen had only been married a year or so and I knew pretty much when they got here that she wasn't happy with the idea.

"Frank Quinn was a local contractor, did okay for himself from what I gathered. But something went wrong. I remember that Dad had talked to him about building the lake house for them, but he decided not to work with Frank when a scandal broke out about his keeping a customer's deposit and not delivering on the job. Construction Industries Commission was breathing down his neck and Dad backed away from working with him. Earleen was in on a lot of those meetings so she knew him back then."

"And she might have felt sorry for his situation."

"Maybe so. I just don't know for sure. Like I said, my life

was pretty full right then. Jake was just getting the research project set up, the grant money out of Harvard, all that. I do know that the same contractor who built Dad's house also did the lab out back."

"What was his name? Maybe he'd remember something."

She squinted upward, remembering. "Mike Roland. Roland Construction. He's got a service yard in that little industrial area about a block past the community center. Lives just down the road from Dad's house. He specializes in luxury homes and really was the right contractor for Dad's place."

"Maybe I'll talk to him. If he was out at your dad's construction site a lot he may have noticed whether Earleen seemed to be up to something."

Amanda's face hardened. "I'd love to find something on her. From day one, I tried to be cordial to her—never really knew what Dad saw in her, but I stayed polite—and she tried to undermine me at every turn. She hated the fact that Dad and I were close and she really didn't want to be living here, so near Jake and me. I still wouldn't be the least bit surprised if she didn't rig the gas leak, just to get rid of the house and get the hell out of Watson's Lake."

She blushed a little after the outburst. "Sorry, I usually don't let personal feelings out that way."

"It's okay. Look, do you mind if I take off? Maybe I can catch Mike Roland before the end of the day."

"Not at all. Let me know how it turns out."

I found the fenced yard of Roland Construction easily enough, right where Amanda'd described it, and I parked on the road to take a look. A chain link fence enclosed about two acres. A long, one-story metal building with four garage doors must have mainly housed tools and materials because two pickup trucks and a cement mixer on a small trailer sat outside. At the near end of the building, a section with windows appeared to be the office (also, a sign with the company logo above the door said so). Everything looked buttoned up tight and I assumed Mike Roland was either out on a job or possibly at home. I was just deciding to drive up toward the Simmons place, in hopes that I could find Mike's home, when I heard a vehicle approach.

The white truck whipped into the driveway and lurched to a stop at the padlocked gate. A tall guy got out, rangy in well-fitted jeans and a T-shirt, his dark hair ruffling in the breeze. He pulled a key from one of those little retractor devices on his belt and applied the key to the padlock. The wide gate rolled back smoothly for him and he got back into the truck and drove it up to the office door. I followed as he unlocked the office door and switched on a light.

"Mike Roland?"

He spun in surprise. "Oh, didn't see you there."

"I'm glad you came along. I'm Charlie Parker, RJP Investigations. We're working with Amanda Zellinger to look into the incident at her father's house a few years ago."

"You were at the funeral this morning, weren't you? Right up front with Amanda?"

"I didn't see you there."

"Well, I wanted to pay my respects but I got this job going out on Lakeview Road, so I couldn't hang around too long. Sorry I missed the graveside part."

I waved it off. "I don't think Amanda necessarily expected everyone to be there."

"How's she doing? I never got to know her too well. She came out to the job site a few times when I built her dad's place, but I guess she's pretty busy. Works at the school, right?" He took a seat behind the desk and indicated the other chair for me.

"Right. She's coping okay. She'd kept her hopes up for four years that her dad would show up alive and well one day, but . . ."

"Yeah, a tough break. I never did buy into that idea that David Simmons would torch that house. He loved the place. We designed it together, you know. He wanted everything just so. The floorplan was his, entirely. The wife got her say in decorating it, but the design and layout was entirely David's."

"So, Earleen wasn't around much during the construction?"

"Well, I didn't say that. She hung out, mostly whenever David came out, which was every day. Walked around and nitpicked little stuff like a crooked nail here and there. No legitimate complaints, really, just being a pain in the butt. Almost every job's got a client like that. Often it's the man, 'cause they think they've gotta exert some control. Wives are usually more interested in what color they're going to choose for the bathroom, whether we should texture the walls or leave them plain for wallpaper. That kind of stuff."

"Amanda said they'd talked to Frank Quinn about bidding the job, but that was about the time his troubles began."

"Troubles." He poofed air through pursed lips. "That's putting it mildly. You don't want to mess with Construction Industries, especially don't want them having any reason to give you the old proctology exam." He blushed. "Sorry, that was a bit graphic."

It didn't bother me, but I caught myself blushing when he did.

He cleared his throat. "Shame, too, because Frank was actually a respected contractor around here for years. Got himself in a bind with some loans and thought he could make it up the quick way. When the client cancelled a job and wanted their deposit back it came out that he hadn't actually put it in an escrow fund at all but had spent it. The stuff hit the fan then, all right."

"I'm surprised he didn't just leave town and start over somewhere else. Go to another state, lie about his past—that kind of thing happens, doesn't it?"

"All the time. I think Frank might have had some other reason to stick around by then."

"Earleen Simmons?"

"Didn't want to say it, but yeah. They were pretty discreet at first. Careful not to flaunt it around David, but the signs were there. I'm out all day in my truck, driving all over this area. Both their cars at the bar at the same time, her car half a block from his house, little stuff. People raised their eyebrows a little but there wasn't anything blatant, not till after David left."

"At what point did she actually move in with Frank?"

He shifted in his chair. "Oh, gosh, few months maybe? I don't know. It's just one of those things that happened. I'm not sure where she stayed right after the house blew up. Seems maybe she went to California for a little bit, but I might be confused about that."

I thanked him for the information, sensing that he'd come back to get some paperwork done before dinnertime and I was keeping him from it. I felt his eyes on my back as I walked back to the Jeep. He'd sent out flirtatious signals but kept eyeing my wedding band and knew I was off limits.

Where had Earleen gone immediately after the fire? I'd have to ask Amanda about that. She'd told the police that she'd been in Santa Fe overnight when the explosion happened; now I wondered if she were with Frank. Might explain why she couldn't produce a receipt for the room, if he'd paid for it.

I circled the block and came out on the main street, west of my motel. As I turned left I passed the Owl Bar and easily spotted Frank's powder-blue car outside. They'd been in there, drinking, for over four hours now. A familiar black Harley sat near the door. I didn't like the looks of that. A sheriff's department cruiser waited across the street, a deputy who appeared to be working a crossword puzzle sat at the wheel and he glanced up as my vehicle went by. I felt better, knowing Michaela had taken me seriously.

In front of my cabin at the Horseshoe I parked and remembered that my Beretta was in the glove compartment. It had seemed like bad form to carry it into the funeral service. I slipped it into my purse and locked the Jeep.

Still satiated with chicken casserole and pineapple upside down cake, I headed for my room with no intention of going out again. It felt good to get out of my dress slacks and the itchy blue sweater that looked good but wore a red spot on my neck. A T-shirt and jeans were much more to my liking. I made a few notes about leads I still wanted to follow, then settled down to an old movie on television.

Although it was a picture I normally loved, an old Ingrid Bergman flick, I couldn't lose myself in the story this time. Earleen's threats at Blythe's office today kept coming back to me. She and Frank were getting desperate. After failing to get the insurance settlement on the house, she'd hoped for half the estate in a divorce, and been thwarted both times. The reading of the will today had clearly come as a total shock to her and she now faced a life of mediocrity in Frank's depressing little house. I took some comfort in the fact that they'd spent the afternoon getting drunk and that a deputy would catch them before they could get out on the road. Abandoning the movie, I picked up the book I'd been reading and did manage to lose myself in it for a couple of hours.

By bedtime I felt more than ready to burrow into the covers for a full eight hours. I'd just drifted off, into that magical realm where sleep occupies ninety-nine percent of consciousness, when the other one percent detected the creak of a floorboard on my porch.

chapter

⇥21⇤

My heart thudded and adrenaline flowed to every cell, bringing me to one hundred percent alert. I froze in position, lying on my side, with my eyes the only body part able to move. The bedside clock showed 10:47. I lifted my head slightly from the pillow, to free up both ears for listening. Another creak sounded, closer to the door. I reached over the edge of the mattress and connected with the strap of my purse which, fortunately, I'd not looped over the chair across the room this time.

The doorknob clicked.

I tugged at the zipper of my bag and reached inside for the Beretta. I flipped off the safety and waited, blinking rapidly to clear my eyes and hoping to pick out shapes in the near-total darkness.

The knob made another small noise, more urgent this time. I'd engaged the chain, but if the intruder managed to get the knob open and if he gave up the pretense at stealth, I knew the chain would accomplish absolutely nothing. I raised the Beretta, knowing the light from the parking area outside would highlight my target for only a few seconds, if I got lucky.

I held my breath.

The knob rattled loudly this time, then I heard the sound of a police siren out on the road. My visitor must have heard it, too, because suddenly the booted feet made two quick steps—not quiet ones—down the porch steps. I whipped the blankets aside and dashed to the window, holding the muzzle of the Beretta toward the floor.

By the light of the mercury vapor lamp in the center of the Horseshoe common, I could barely make out a running figure that disappeared between two cabins on the opposite side. I debated giving chase and gave up the thought in about two-tenths of a second. I'm not fond of putting my life on the line. Plus, I sleep in only a T-shirt and panties. The town of Watson's Lake did not need that to talk about in the morning.

In the distance, I heard a vehicle start, but it could have been anyone. I debated calling the sheriff's office but decided to wait and mention it some other time. I'd already racked up a couple of favors from Michaela and didn't want her to start ignoring me because I came across as some female scaredy-cat.

I went back to bed and found myself listening for sounds until four o'clock. The Beretta didn't make a very comfortable bed partner but I wasn't about to let it out of my reach. As gray light began to appear at the window's edge, sometime around five, I drifted off to sleep. When I awoke at eight, the events during the night seemed almost unreal and I half wondered whether I'd imagined them. Not a reassuring thought, since I'd lost a whole night's sleep for nothing, if that were the case.

I dragged myself to the shower then dressed in fresh jeans and a clean cotton sweater, determined to start this day with a purpose. I had people to see and things to do. And I wanted to get finished here within a few days so Drake and I might spend next weekend together. As I bent forward to dry my hair I read back over the notes I'd made last night, then stuck the little notepad back into my purse.

Breakfast first. The early crowd at Jo's should be gone and who knew, maybe I'd pick up some tidbit about whether the sheriff had actually nabbed Frank and Earleen last night for attempting to drive home intoxicated. I debated carrying the Beretta with me—it really weighed down my purse—and decided I should. I have a permit for it and shouldn't be afraid to protect myself. I swung the strap of the purse over my shoulder and headed toward Jo's.

She'd already figured out that my usual routine was to finish one whole cup of coffee before ordering, another while they prepared my food, and to linger over the meal with a third. The minute I took a seat the first cup appeared.

"Hear about the excitement last night?" she said as she poured.

I could immediately think of two possibilities but decided it was wiser not to vocalize them. I let her go on.

"The burglary out at the Handy Mart?"

I guess I looked totally blank.

"Two guys came in awhile after closing, like midnight. Took off with the cash, which stupid Debbie Gibbons didn't put in the safe. Said nothing ever happens, so she just left it in the drawer. Got away with a bunch of music CDs too, and a carton of Twinkies that were right beside the register. Set off the silent alarm, which everybody in this town knows about, and by the time Michaela's deputy got there they were gone. They're calling them the Twinkie Bandits, you know, 'cause of the Twinkies."

"Cute."

"So, anyway, this deputy that was supposed to be keeping an eye out for the drunks leaving the Owl, he's not at his post and Frank Quinn managed to have a fender bender on the way home. Guess him and Earleen'd been drinking all afternoon and all night, so it's amazing they only hit a lamp post. They got citations and would've had to sleep it off in County but there was nobody available to drive 'em over there so Michaela let 'em go home, but she took away Frank's keys."

She wrote down my order, a cheese omelet, and another customer caught her attention. "Makes me glad I don't serve booze," she said as she walked away.

So Frank and Earleen weren't being watched as they left the bar, and it must have been sometime around midnight. I thought again of the figure I'd seen running from my cabin, but wouldn't bet on it being Frank. I wouldn't imagine he could be that steady on his feet after the amount of alcohol he must have consumed. And besides, the timing didn't quite fit.

Jo was busy with a late mini-rush when I got ready to leave so I left money on the counter and skipped the third cup of coffee. It's way more than I ever drink at home anyway, a good time to start cutting back. I walked back to the Horseshoe with a fresh eye toward finding out if the guy who'd run away from my door last night had evil intentions. With everything else going on in town, certainly no law enforcement person had been around to notice.

There'd been no rain in more than a week, so a nicely defined footprint in the mud was more than I could hope for. Lots of blurred ones showed up in the dust near the road, the pathway that I usually took, myself, when I walked to and from Jo's. The driveways and parking areas inside the Horseshoe common area were neatly graveled and the grass at the center was getting a little longish. No prints there.

I noticed that the dusty surface of my tiny porch looked disturbed, but if a print showed up it would probably be mine or the maid's. I climbed the two steps and rummaged for my key. That's when a glint of something shiny caught my attention. Lying in the grass at the base of the steps, the object only caught the light at a certain angle. The gleaming silver part was a blade. And the handle—I'd seen it before. The Harley-Davidson logo stood out distinctively.

I ducked back down the steps and reached for it, holding back at the last second. Maybe the crime scene people should photograph it in place. What crime scene people? Charlie, you watch too much TV. In this town I'd be lucky to get an officer who would actually come to the cabin and take a statement. Still, I didn't want to mess up any remote possibility to get Rocko Rodman hauled away.

I pulled my cell phone from my purse and dialed the sheriff's office. Michaela was out on calls, I learned, but the dispatcher would send her over here. The woman wasn't sure how soon it would be, as the sheriff was working a big burglary case this morning. The hint of pride in her voice let me know that the Handy Mart robbery was a pretty big deal for this town. I stared down at the knife again.

The idea that Rocko Rodman had stood outside my door with this weapon unsheathed last night, that he'd actually tried the doorknob, sent a chill over my arms. I lost any uneasiness I'd felt over pulling my Beretta. This guy was evil.

I unlocked my cabin door and went inside for a jacket. Suddenly the May morning held little warmth. I felt antsy. I couldn't just sit on the step, staring at the knife, until Michaela came. But I couldn't let it out of my sight either. My leg twitched with impatience and I finally decided to walk off some of the excess energy. I stashed my purse out of sight and closed the cabin, then strode down the steps and followed the drive-way. As long as I kept the cabin in sight, no one could come along and remove the evidence.

The ten cabins ringed the horseshoe-shaped common, quiet this morning in their setting of tall pines. All had been occupied last night, but nearly everyone had already checked out this morning. Number four's occupants were just now hauling their bags to their car, preparing to leave, and number six's people looked like they planned to stay. I noted that the maid had only reached number two so far, so she wouldn't get around to my place for another hour or more.

I fast-walked the gravel oval twice and felt calmer for it. One more time, and maybe I'd hear something from the sheriff by then. I'd reached the gap between cabins two and three when it occurred to me that this was the spot where my visitor had fled. I paused, still watching for Michaela's cruiser at any minute, and sized up the scene.

The grass was beaten down between the cabins, but this was far more traffic than one man, running through one time, would have caused. Prints would probably be impossible to get. Number three had a small window facing the gap, and

I guessed it corresponded to the bathroom of that unit, since mine had the same style window there. Unless someone inside had made a midnight bathroom run at that moment and . . . No, there's no way they would have seen anything through the frosted glass.

I walked through the gap and noticed that the rear of the cabins would have provided a pretty good spot to park a vehicle out of sight. The huge pines grew tightly together and beyond them was the service road the gas company truck probably used to access a monstrous propane tank at the back of the property. I glanced back at my cabin. If a vehicle were left here, the man running away could have hopped in and driven away. I'd heard something start up in the night; could have come from this spot. I'd show it to Michaela when she arrived.

I turned back to my cabin, deciding I might just have to sit on the porch after all, when the sun sparkled off something at my feet. A Twinkie wrapper.

A vehicle sound caught my attention and I looked up to see the brown and gold cruiser pulling up to my cabin, across the common.

"Michaela," I shouted when she emerged. I waved her over. "Looks pretty new, don't you think?"

She picked up the wrapper with the tips of her nails and turned it around to look at it from all angles. "Couldn't have been out here more than a day. No dust on it at all."

"Could go with last night's robbery," I said as she carried it back to her cruiser and located a paper bag to put the wrapper in.

"I'm wondering if this also goes with last night's robbery, now," I told her as I pointed out the Harley-Davidson knife.

She hunkered down and stared at it without touching it. "It's Rocko's. I'd bet on that anyway. It's been among his possessions every time I've hauled him in."

I told her about the midnight intruder on my porch and how he'd tried the door. I left out the part about how I'd intended to blow him away if he'd actually opened it.

"He ran off between the two cabins where we just got the wrapper," I said. "Don't you think it's entirely possible that he and Billy knocked off the Handy Mart, then Billy waited at his truck and had a little snack while Rocko decided to pay me a visit?"

"I'd say it's possible. But what's Rocko's motive? Why'd he come after you?"

"For starters, I'd guess that he's not too happy that I turned him in for the hit and run on Amanda Zellinger. He did a few days in jail for that."

"If Rocko Rodman went after everyone who'd ever had a hand in his going to jail, half the town'd be dead."

I repressed the smart remark I'd been about to utter.

She proceeded to stick the knife in an evidence bag and made some notes about my story.

"What's it going to take to put the Rodman brothers away permanently?" I asked. "What happened to 'three strikes you're out'?" I felt my face going red as I heated up.

"Look, it's not up to me. I arrest 'em, send 'em up to Segundo. Judge up there just happens to be one of the most liberal in the state and she seems to think they can be rehabilitated. There's an abysmal recidivism rate up here and it's beyond me how the lady keeps getting re-elected, but she does. Talk to the voters."

I fumed but realized the futility of it.

When Michaela drove away I stood there, watching the cruiser make a left turn onto Main Street. I knew she'd do her duty once more, arrest the Rodman brothers and send them up for prosecution. And for a small-town, grandmotherly sheriff that was about all she could do. I gritted my teeth, almost wishing Rocko had gotten into my cabin with his knife in hand. He wouldn't be going back to the kindly judge in Segundo today, that's for sure.

Inside my little room, I flopped into the overstuffed chair for a couple of minutes but got bored with that almost immediately. Drop the Rodman issues, Charlie. Get back to Amanda's situation. I pulled out my notes from the previous day and read over them.

The question had come up about Earleen's whereabouts right after the fire. Where had she stayed once her own home was gone, before she moved in with Frank Quinn? Amanda might remember.

If Earleen had been involved with Frank during her marriage to David, would it make sense that she was insanely jealous enough of Bettina to target her? I kept coming back to that unanswered question: who was the real target? David, Earleen, or Bettina? And depending on the answer to that, who had motive enough?

Jealousy loomed as one likely reason, and I could apply it in equal measure to several people, but the crime itself didn't seem to fit. If Earleen were jealous of Bettina, she could have surely just managed to run the poor girl out of town. She surely wouldn't destroy her own home for that reason. David's jealousy over an affair between his wife and Frank Quinn might have spurred the desire to blow up something, but then who killed David? Rocko was hot-headed enough to do just about anything, but I saw him as more the catch-'em-in-a-dark-alley type. Having the finesse to break into the house undetected, rig the gas to explode, and wait for David to come home—nah. He'd simply have waited for David and bashed him over the head. And that might be exactly what happened.

The other big motivator in all this seemed to be money. David, particularly, had been obsessed with it. Moving it around, borrowing here, stashing it there. Doing his best to hide it from Earleen. And it was certainly a motivator for her, the reason she'd married him in the first place. Jake and Amanda were strapped. Frank Quinn had known better times and had quite likely hooked up with Earleen in some hope of regaining them.

Combine both motives—money and jealousy—and I could be looking at just about anything. I closed the notebook and shoved it back into my purse. I felt time running out. Amanda would be going back to work soon, getting on with real life. She'd buried her father and would need to put the past behind her. The sheriff's department and state police would keep working the murder case, but others would come along and this one would slip to the bottom of the stack, then the cold case file, and eventually the archives. If I didn't come across any new evidence within a week, I might as well pack up and go home.

My cell phone rang as I was starting the Jeep, planning to drive to Amanda's.

"Just to let you know," said Michaela. "We've been questioning the Rodman boys and it looks like your hunch was right. They'd planned to teach you a little lesson about turning them in for the hit-and-run. Rocko's been ranting for an hour—right up to the minute we put him into a squad car headed for County. He won't get out for at least a month, but no guarantees what that judge'll do. You ought to watch your back."

"And Billy?"

"He's on his way out too. Not quite as hot-tempered as Rocko, but he's no angel, either. We've got him for the Handy Mart."

I clicked off the call with an uneasy knot in my gut. I pulled in at the Horseshoe office and asked Selena if I could be put in a different cabin. There weren't many choices of motels in this town, but I'd do what I could, including parking my car by the office instead of at my own front door.

By the time I got to Amanda's I'd calmed down quite a bit, but she noticed. I got into a short explanation of the night's events and the fact that the Rodmans were again on their way to jail.

"Sheriff Michaela told me they blame me for turning them in on your accident. They claim they'd just had a little too much to drink and it was nothing personal toward you. They think they did enough time for it."

She paused with a dripping mug that she'd been about to

put into the dishwasher, in mid-air. "That ridiculous! Those two have caused problems in this town for years."

"Don't even get me started. I had this discussion with the sheriff already. She says we need to convince the voters not to re-elect that district judge." I felt my blood pressure rising again and quelled the urge to rant on.

Amanda jammed the last few pieces into the dishwasher, slopped powdered soap across the door, closed it, and dialed in the setting she wanted. As it began to hum she dried her hands and tapped the button on the intercom. "Ready, Jake," she said.

"We're heading into town," she said. "I need to stop at the bank and Jake needs something from the hardware store. Want to ride along?"

I'd wanted to ask a few questions, and maybe it would be helpful to have both of them captive at once.

"I hope my auto insurance comes through soon. This business of having only one car is getting a little cumbersome and it's going to get worse next week when I go back to work. Jake may have to drive me there and pick me up. With the erratic schedule I have, meetings, and in-service days, he's not going to be happy about that."

"I thought you had the whole month off," I said as I trailed along. She buzzed through the house, switching off lights and gathering purse and papers.

"No point in sitting here and thinking about everything. I'm getting calls again from that mortgage company on the two million dollar loan." Her voice got tight.

"Dad's life insurance did come through quickly, though. I was surprised." She held up an envelope. "I'd like to tap into it for a new car but between Jake's work and the debts I don't know."

Jake met us at the Mazda and he took the wheel. I buckled into the back and held on as he whipped out onto the road. Seemed as though his youthful appearance translated to youthful habits, too. We made it into town in record time and I didn't get a chance to pose my question about Earleen because the two of them chatted about their errands during the short ride. Jake stopped at the bank first and Amanda went in.

"How's the work coming along?" I asked, more as a way to make conversation than anything.

"Really well," he said. "I'm shipping the final design work to my manufacturer right now, in fact." He held up a tube mailer that I hadn't noticed earlier.

"What's your time-frame after that?"

"Few weeks to see the final prototype. We've made two already, done modifications. Hoping this will be the magic one. We'll use it to make the final presentation to the East Coast group, and with their blessing we hope to go into production."

"That's great. And the implant you did on yourself? That's working as it should, I guess?"

He started to answer but cut it off when Amanda opened her door. I wondered if these two really communicated much at all.

"No immediate visit to the car dealership," she said. "They say there'll be a week's hold on the funds, because of the amount."

Jake didn't look happy about this, and she fumed a bit. I knew it for standard procedure in banking; holding funds was a great way for them to earn sizeable interest. Even a few days float on a half-million dollars added up.

Jake gunned the engine as he roared out of the bank lot and jack-rabbited the SUV two blocks to his next stop, the post office. Amanda and I waited while he went inside.

"Guess I shouldn't have mentioned that," she said. "But I know he wants to start writing checks right away. He's going to have to fly to Boston next week, too. Oh, well, there are always credit cards."

I wasn't sure what to say to that so I changed the subject. "Tell me more about Bettina. I'm trying to make the connections between all the relationships in your dad's case. I heard a rumor that they may have had a fling."

She turned to face me. "That's ridiculous, Charlie. I know about the rumors. People never said anything to me directly, but they gossiped a lot right after the fire. I'd walk into a room and conversation would just go dead. I know they were talking about my dad. Yes, he and Bettina got together a few times. But it was not sexual. They met at our house several times and I was right there. I'd tutored Bettina to complete her GED and Dad was trying to help her get a scholarship for college, for god's sake. He felt sorry for her. She'd gotten a bad start here and her past just wouldn't leave her alone.

"Guys came on to her all the time. That poor girl put up with it but she was humiliated. Dad thought a person shouldn't have to live with their youthful mistakes forever. He told her she could get into college, somewhere in another city, make a new start. She had the grades for it, just needed the financial help. I sat right there while they filled out the applications."

I felt a flush rise on my face. I'd bought into the rumor far too easily. "I'm glad you told me. Why doesn't that rumor get around town, instead of the negative one?"

"What good would it do now? Bettina died four years ago. There's no way to go back and recreate her life. Michaela was about the only other person who cared for her. She's done a pretty good job of shutting people up, but even she didn't know about the girl's hopes for a better education."

"I'm sorry to hear it."

Jake returned then and we fell silent. So, if the Bettina-David affair was non-existent, there went some of the motive. Surely, David would have at least given the real story to his own wife. But what about Bettina's boyfriend at the time, Rocko? That guy probably wouldn't listen to reason, even if he'd known. He may not have felt jealous of David, per se. Maybe his jealousy stemmed from the fact that Bettina actually had a way out of Watson's Lake and a chance at a better life. Rocko may've imagined the two of them together forever and decided if he couldn't have her, she could forget any other options.

❧ 22 ❧

The hardware store was located next to Jo's, and Amanda and I decided to have a cup of tea while Jake shopped. He'd already said it might take awhile. Jo greeted us and raised the coffee pot with a question on her face, surprised when I turned that down and asked for tea instead.

"You ladies want a pastry to go with those?" she asked when she brought mugs and little pots of hot water.

We both shook our heads.

"I wanted to ask you about Earleen again," I said, dunking my teabag a half-dozen times. "I never did hear where she went immediately after the fire. With her home gone, did she rent a place?"

Amanda finished her own teabag ritual and poured. "Let me think. I was in shock, myself, and not paying a lot of attention to her. It seems like she was gone for a few days, and I think she told me she went to California. There's a sister or cousin or somebody there. She must have stayed with them for a bit. I'm not sure."

"At what point did she move in with Frank? I guess what I'm getting at is, were they fooling around at that point or did he come along later?"

"My opinion? I think something had been going on for awhile. I told you he'd been one of the contractors asked to bid on the house? Yeah, well when it became obvious that Dad wouldn't want to work with him, Frank didn't exactly go away. He found reasons to be around the job and there were little signals zipping back and forth between him and Earleen. How far it went, I can't say."

"I wonder if she'd admit to that now."

She gave a little snorting chuckle. "I doubt that. You know how history tends to get rewritten. I'm sure by now she's convinced herself that she was the perfect, faithful wife. She could probably say that on a polygraph and get away with it."

"I'm just having a hard time imagining Frank's appeal. Especially when she already had David and knew he was building that fabulous house."

"Frank was different then. He'd been successful for several years. And he spent freely, wore nice clothes, drove a brand new Suburban. He presented a way better picture than he does now."

I digested all that. It made sense. Part of Frank's appeal, in some skewed way, might have been Earleen's disillusionment with her husband. He'd made the decision about their move to Watson's Lake and about his heavy financial investment in Jake's research. A new man, one who concentrated his attention on her, and her alone, might have been the thing to turn Earleen's head. No matter that the guy was dishonest and essentially a loser. David hadn't exactly been forthright with her either.

My cell phone rang as Jo came around with offers to refill our tea pots. Amanda agreed and I nodded as I checked the caller ID. Ron.

"Let me take this outside where it's a little quieter," I said.

"What's up?" he said when I answered.

"Many things, but no answers," I told him. "Any news on the insurance?"

"That's what I was calling about. Finally got through to the guy who'd agreed to research it for me. No deal. Continental Union isn't going to pay on the house as long as there's an unsolved arson case on the property. They're still adamant that David might have set it up and if the homeowner was involved in any way, no payment."

Then the mortgage company would be breathing down Amanda's neck. They certainly wouldn't take the loss.

"I'm asking a lot of questions," I told him, "and it's getting interesting. I'm trying to concentrate on the arson, since the police are more focused on David's murder at this point. But there are so many twists and tangles to the motives, I'm not sure I'm accomplishing much."

"And, let me guess, Amanda's money is running out?"

"Not entirely. David's life insurance did pay off. But I don't know how much of it she wants to devote to this. I'm planning to ask her."

I did just that when I returned to the table. In low tones, she debated it.

"I don't know, Charlie. I want to know, of course. But I'm not sure how much to spend. We really need every cent at this point. Until Jake's product goes to market and starts to bring in something."

"I understand. We've pretty well gone through the retainer you gave me. How about this? I stay until the end of the week, three more days. If I can find the answer and you end up collecting the insurance, you pay me. If not, no obligation."

She bestowed a relieved smile on me. "Thanks."

What she didn't know was that I knew the whereabouts of a ton of money that would probably rightfully be hers. So many tangled strings were attached, though, that I didn't want to mention it just yet.

Jake popped his head in the door. "Manda, gotta go."

It wasn't actually a request, and she jumped up like he'd pushed her On button. I dropped a few bills on the table and we got into the car as he was putting it in gear.

"Those men from Med-Accept will be here any time," he said when Amanda opened her mouth to question the abrupt departure.

"This early? That's the company that'll market Jake's device once the prototype tests are done," she said over her shoulder.

"This is probably the most important meeting I'll have all year," he said, "along with the Harvard group next week." He reached over and squeezed Amanda's hand.

A gray sedan sat in their driveway when we pulled up and Jake immediately tensed. "Oh, geez." Three men in suits were standing at the front door, looking like they were wondering what to do now that they hadn't gotten an answer.

Amanda patted his shoulder. "Don't worry. Bring them into the house and I'll offer coffee or lunch. We'll get them relaxed and then you can take them out to the lab."

He took a deep breath. "Okay."

Amanda played perfect hostess as she walked up to the men and introduced everyone. Jake's assurance in the lab didn't quite translate to personal encounters. I could see where David's skill with people had gone a long way in the business aspects of their mutual project."

She ushered the men into the living room, which I noticed for the first time was immaculate. After ascertaining that they'd already had lunch but would love coffee, she and I exited to the kitchen and left the men to talk. She pulled out a special Hawaiian blend and started the brewer. A bakery box came out of the pantry and she arranged cookies on a plate. Fine china came out of a cabinet near the table and a silver tray held cups and saucers. When the coffee finished brewing, she took the tray and I held the cookie plate.

"...at this point, the patent documents are the only sticking point," one of the men was saying. I think he'd introduced himself as Walter Cassman.

"You've got them, right?" the tall guy called Brian Wickfield asked.

Amanda bustled in just then, distracting them with the coffee, offering cream and sugar, serving each man in turn.

I noticed a thin sheen of sweat on Jake's forehead and wondered about that.

"We'll go out to the lab in a couple minutes," he said, taking the cup Amanda handed him. When the cup rattled against the saucer he subtly shifted it back to her and reached for a cookie instead. "Um, hon, these are great. My mom's recipe?"

She smiled and avoided an answer by passing the plate among the others. The conversation veered toward the deliciousness of the cookies and a discussion of the Hawaiian coffee, reminding Wickfield what a great time he and his wife had enjoyed on the Big Island last summer.

I ducked into the kitchen to grab the coffee carafe, wondering about Jake's sudden nervousness. He'd talked as if the patent was a done deal, so what was the hang up? I chalked it up to general anxiety that the deal go through and his youth and inexperience with this part of the process.

Amanda took the pot from me and refilled. I hovered in the kitchen, not wanting to make an issue of leaving, but eager to get going. The clinking of cups being set down and the return to business conversation signaled a change, and the four males came through the kitchen on their way to the lab out back. Jake would be in his element when he got them out there.

I left the kitchen cleanup to her and drove back to town. I had three days to try and figure out the arson situation and didn't want to waste any time. The problem was that I felt stymied and wasn't sure where to turn next. I knew Continental Union would surely have their own investigators and their job would be to try to save the company two million dollars by denying the claim. If Amanda had any hope at all, it was going to be with me.

A brown and gold cruiser sat at one of the pumps at Woody's Chevron and I pulled in behind it.

"Yes, the sheriff even has to pump her own gas," Michaela said when I approached. "I do get a county credit card to pay for it, though." She gave me a long stare. "Gassing up to head home?" she asked.

I heard the hope in her voice and ignored it. "I'm still on the job." I walked close enough to her that our voices wouldn't carry. "Michaela, is there some reason you don't like David's family? I get these strong vibes that you had no regard whatsoever for David, and you haven't exactly been cooperative with Amanda either."

Her jaw tightened and a muscle quivered near her ear.

"I don't know this family," I said. "I just came into the middle and I'm checking out possibilities. That's all. If they're terrible people, let me know. I haven't seen it."

She struggled with something, glanced down at the badge on her ample chest. "As a law enforcement officer, I suppose I'm pretty much in the same boat you are. I've looked at this arson case every which way and, other than the insurance motive, can't find any proof positive." She replaced the gas nozzle and closed the cap on her vehicle before speaking again. "As a person, I just didn't happen to care much for David Simmons. His . . . values . . . didn't correspond with mine."

"You're talking about the alleged affair with Bettina?"

"Everybody knew it. They spent way more time together than a married man and a young woman should do."

"Did you ever actually take the time to ask your niece about this relationship? I know you cared for her. Did you find out what they were doing?"

"We didn't talk often, not about personal matters."

"Maybe you should have. Maybe she would have told you that David was helping her apply for financial aid to college. Maybe she would have told you that Amanda tutored her and helped her with her GED."

Michaela couldn't meet my gaze now.

"Maybe 'poor little Bettina' wanted something better for herself than this town and Rocko Rodman as the man in her life. No one here would take her seriously but she hoped to make a new start in a new place."

"I . . . whew! I never saw that." She shuffled a ring of keys from one hand to the other. She rubbed a hand across her forehead and fluffed her bangs. "Maybe I am getting too old for this job."

I relaxed the set of my shoulders. "I didn't mean it that way," I said. "I didn't know it either and I made the same judgments. Maybe it's a lesson in keeping an open mind."

"So, what's this mean overall to the investigation."

"I don't know," I admitted. "I'd like to think it takes away someone's motive, but if everyone in town thought the same thing, it doesn't matter that it wasn't true. I'm still leaning toward Rocko, although I'm not sure he had the smarts to set everything up. It seems more likely that he'd simply batter Bettina a bit and wait somewhere in the dark for David."

"Which he may very well have done."

"But would he take the time and trouble to figure out how to sink the car and cover up the evidence?"

She leaned against the cruiser. "I always figured Amanda herself as a possibility." She held up a hand to my automatic protest. "Just keep that open mind for a minute. No love lost between her and Earleen. She knew her father was going out of town, knew Earleen would get home the next day and be there alone. She's intelligent."

"As open as I'd like to be on this, I just don't see Amanda taking a violent path. She'd be more of a poisoner, don't you think?" We both managed to crack a smile at that. "Seriously, she would have known which were Bettina's housekeeping days and would have never done anything to harm her."

"Good point." She selected a key from the ring and reached for the car door. "Well, it's been real informative."

"You don't mind my staying around for a few more days then?"

She gave a shrug. "Have at it."

I realized I needed to pee worse than anything in the world and the greasy condition of Woody's shop interior didn't bode well. The Horseshoe was such a short distance away that I hopped in the Jeep and drove over. I almost pulled up in front of Cabin 10 when I remembered that Selena had switched keys with me this morning and I was moving into number two. I dashed in and used the facilities. Relieved, I went back out to the car and brought in my lone duffle bag and purse. I'm not the kind of traveler who moves lock, stock, and barrel into a motel. It had taken all of three minutes to load up, and now it took less than two to do my usual minimal unpacking.

Michaela had succeeded in one thing; she'd made me consider Amanda and Earleen's rivalry. Not that I believed for a second that Amanda had what it took to bring herself to blow up her father's house. She simply didn't seem vindictive enough or focused enough. I felt sure her fourth graders loved her fuzzy demeanor and faint driftiness. It made her likeable. But she'd have to be hiding a lot more steel somewhere in her petite frame to plan and carry out arson and murder.

That said, I still had to consider that if there was one person in the world Amanda hated enough to kill, it was Earleen. And the feeling was mutual.

Perhaps another visit with the widow would be in order. I cruised past Frank's house, saw no vehicle out front, and tapped on the door anyway. Maybe Earleen was home alone. No such luck. Frank answered, clearly freshly up from an interrupted nap, and he mumbled something about where she'd gone. I didn't catch it before he closed the door. I didn't stay around to find out more.

I drove past the elementary school, circled by the bank and grocery, past Jo's. No sign of the Olds. Cutting in past the community center, I took the parallel street to the north and spotted a flash of powder blue in the next block. The Olds was parked in front of Billy Rodman's house and I braked the minute I realized it.

The brothers should still be in jail. I sincerely hoped their friendly judge hadn't set a bond they could meet, since this time the crime involved a sizeable burglary and attempted break in. Surely the evidence of the knife near my cabin door would hold them awhile.

⇥23⇤

W hile all this ran through my head, I spotted movement at the front door. Earleen, wearing a brilliant orange and lime green top and orange leggings, stepped out and turned to lock the door with a key. I eased up behind the Olds, cut the engine, and got out.

"Hi there," I said.

She started and shot me a look when she realized who'd spoken. "What do you want?"

What did I want? Did I expect her to admit her hatred for Amanda was strong enough that she'd gone to great lengths to blow up her own house? That didn't make a lot of sense. I remembered Michaela's initial suspicions and took a different tactic.

"I get the feeling Amanda never did think much of you."

She snorted. "You go to college to figure that out?"

"Did she hate you enough to burn down your house, you think? Maybe she even hoped you'd be home when it happened."

"Look, chickie, chumpy, whatever your name is, you're on the wrong track with me. I have no idea what goes on in that girl's head. Never did. I tried, I really tried to 'bond' with her in the beginning. She was already David's grown daughter, but I thought we might have some kind of family life. The little b--, girl, didn't like me from day one and there was no changing her mind."

She bounced her weight from one leg to the other and rested a hand on one hip. "Since the fire she's done nothing for me. Nothing to help me with a few extra bucks now and then, nothing to console me over the loss of my husband. Well, you can have her. As far as I'm concerned, it's too bad Rocko didn't hit her car harder that night."

I glanced toward the house.

"Oh, no. Not what you're thinking. I just come over to feed the dog whenever they're gone."

She said it as if Rocko and Billy were on vacation somewhere. Guess it was more like a business trip.

"There's nothing personal here," she said.

"But you must be friends?"

"We catch a drink or two now and then. They hang out at the Owl, so do Frank and me. That's that."

And how easy it would be to let the local thugs know that somebody's a real thorn in your side and you'd like to be rid of her. And how convenient that after a few drinks these two guys can just claim DWI rather than attempted murder. I watched Earleen climb behind the wheel of the big old boat and give the engine three cranks before it started. A puff of black exhaust whoofed out at me and I turned my back, waving my hand in front of my face. I hoped she saw me in her mirror.

Once the air cleared, I got back into the Jeep and drove slowly back toward the Horseshoe. I realized I hadn't eaten anything since breakfast and was running on empty. Considering the nearly sleepless night and discovery of Rocko's weapon outside my door, it was amazing I was still functional at all. I stopped at Jo's where I went the full-fat route with a chicken-fried steak, cream gravy, and potatoes. For dessert there was no holding me back from the cherry cobbler.

I waddled out to the car and drove it the fifty yards to the motel. Parking near the office, to obscure the location of my cabin, I locked up and went to the room. I tried to lie down and read, but my full stomach grumbled and everything felt like it was charging back up my throat. Like it or not, I needed to move around before I settled down for the night. I put on my walking shoes and did four laps' walk around the common area.

Okay, they were slow laps but at least I moved about until my food began to digest.

Back in the room I read in the comfy chair—identical to the one I'd had in my other cabin—until I simply couldn't keep my eyes open. The third time I caught my head bobbing, I got up and brushed my teeth. By the time I'd slipped out of my clothes and into the bed, I was yawning hugely.

I knew nothing else until the sun came through my window at seven the next morning. I woke and stretched, giving myself a few minutes of sheer laziness before starting the day. I realized that I didn't actually have a plan for the day but, knowing that inaction breeds inaction, I got up and brushed my teeth and showered. Last night's dinner hung stubbornly with me and I found I couldn't think about food. I breakfasted on a cup of tea that I brewed in the room.

Flipping through the pages in my little notebook, I looked for loose ends. Something was eluding me and I couldn't seem to put my finger on it. I phoned Michaela to see if she'd share anything about the murder investigation.

"Our department is working with the state police on this one, Charlie," she said. "We're the little guys and are lucky to get any crumbs ourselves. I can tell you that they're pretty sure they've got the murder weapon though."

My interest perked.

"A tire iron. It was in the backseat of David's car, like somebody'd tossed it there. Makes sense. The guy bashes David over the head and knows he's going to get rid of the body and the car. Might as well send the weapon over the edge with it."

"Any prints? Evidence?"

"Unfortunately, no. If there were, originally, anything like that's long gone now. Interesting thing, though, the weapon's not David's. Doesn't match his car at all. The state folks are tracing it now, seeing if they can match it up to a specific make and model. It may not lead anywhere; those things can be pretty generic. We'll see."

I hung up, pondering this. We could eliminate any vehicle newer than four years. That could be a good thing or a bad thing. If whoever did this had bought a new car, it would be next to impossible to make any positive connection between the tire iron and a car they probably traded in long ago.

Among the suspects who still drove their older cars were certainly Frank Quinn and Billy Rodman. I'd pretty much bet money that neither of them had traded vehicles in the past four years. And Rocko certainly had access to his brother's truck almost any time. That brought me back to the incident two nights ago, when it seemed clear that Rocko Rodman had approached my cabin. Remembering that knife lying in the grass beside the steps still gave me a little chill.

The brothers were in the county jail in Segundo right now. I'd given a statement to Michaela but wondered whether it would reinforce the case against them if I also spoke with someone there.

Without a better plan for the day, I gathered what I'd need and drove north. The town was slightly less busy, mid-morning, mid-week. I recognized a few landmarks like the Wal-Mart store, and remembered the place we'd turned to go to Horton Blythe's office. I didn't know the town layout at all, but figured it couldn't be that hard. I kept going toward what felt like the center of town, and spotted signs that pointed toward City Hall, County Courthouse, and Public Library.

At the courthouse, I asked about the Sheriff's Department and was told they were located in a separate building about a block away. I could walk through the jail annex and into a parking lot, the clerk said, and cut through there. It would be quicker and easier than trying to find another parking spot. Considering that it had taken me ten minutes to find the one I got, I took that as good advice. What was with this place, anyway? The government offices were more popular than Wal-Mart, it seemed.

As I entered the jail annex, I had to pass through a metal

detector and by a desk where a uniformed guard sat. Luckily, I'd remembered to lock the Beretta back in my glove compartment.

"Here to visit a prisoner?" she asked in a bored monotone.

"Uh, no." I glanced at the crowded room and realized I must have just hit visiting hours. I recoiled slightly from the noise and the smell of unwashed bodies and dirty diapers. The crowd, women mostly, many with young children hanging onto them, sat on benches rimming the walls, apparently waiting for their turns.

"Not visiting?" the guard said. "What's your business then?"

The first clerk hadn't told me there would be a Q & A session here. I started to tell her that I just wanted to pass through but an idea hit me.

"Uh, I am, actually. I'd like to speak with Rocko Rodman. Oh wait, that's George Rodman."

She flipped through some sheets in a notebook, asked to see my ID, and wrote something down.

"You get this back when you leave," she said, clearly amused at my lack of knowledge, as she tucked my driver's license into a small file box.

Like I was going to pass my license through to Rocko and he would use it—how, exactly?

Oh well, now I was stuck. I walked into the crowd and edged my way to a clear spot on the wall. A baby started screaming next to me and the mother bounced him on her hip. I was about to go back and tell the guard I'd just forget the visit when another guard appeared and called off a bunch of names. About half the women stood up and followed him. I heard him say "Ten minutes" a few times as they began to file through the doorway. I looked at my watch.

If they called the same number of names next time, I should be in the next group, ten minutes from now, and out of here in twenty. That was doable.

When our turn came to file in, I got behind a weary-looking woman in a pair of low-cut jeans and a T-shirt that was about three sizes too small. She'd clearly done the drill a lot in her life-time so I followed her moves. We came into a large room with tables set in a U shape. Prisoners in orange jump suits sat around the inner perimeter of the U, and the women began filling in the spaces opposite them. I recognized Rocko and stepped over to his spot. There was no glass between prisoner and vis-itor, but four guards posted themselves at strategic places and I didn't figure it was too likely that Rodman would attempt to jump the table and rip my throat out.

He visibly started when he saw that I was his visitor.

"Who were you expecting?" I asked, determined to stay cool, even though my heart was pounding erratically and I'd seriously begun to question my sanity. I sat back in my chair, keeping well out of arm's reach.

His eyes narrowed and he didn't respond.

"You dropped your knife outside my cabin the other night. What were you doing there?"

He tried to ignore that one, too, his face sullen.

"That's okay. I've moved now. The evidence speaks for itself. I really didn't come here to ask you about that, anyway. I wanted to talk to you about Bettina."

He shifted in his seat. I imagined a slight softening in his posture.

"You'd been dating quite a awhile before she died?"

He shrugged. "Few months."

"Was it serious? I mean, did she confide things to you?"

"Sure."

I felt like I needed a can opener to get this guy to open up.

"Things, like her feelings about David? The things they talked about sometimes?"

Fire came into his eyes then. "She wasn't never gonna be with him. She loved me." He stabbed a finger onto the table top. "Me!"

As his voice rose, a guard took a step closer.

"She worked a couple of days a week for David and

Earleen," I said. "Were they regular days? Or did she just go over there whenever the place needed cleaning?"

"What are you getting at? She loved me. She didn't want that guy David and if he came on to her, I'd have killed him." He stopped abruptly, his words echoing in one of those strange moments when it seems all conversation stops.

I stared at him until the other buzz in the room started up again. "Did you kill him, Rocko? Did you follow through on that?"

He gave me a frigid stare that sent goosebumps up my arms. "Guard!" he shouted. "We done here."

He stood and turned his back on me, letting the guard escort him through a doorway on the other side of the room. As he reached the door, he turned and flashed a malevolent stare at me. I rubbed at my prickly arms as I stood.

Out in the lobby, I retrieved my license and asked how long the Rodman brothers would be inside. The clerk at the desk looked up something on a computer.

"Arraignment's this afternoon," she said. "Depends on whether they post bond. If not, hearing's on Friday and they'll set a trial date."

"Who's the judge for the bond hearing?"

"Judge Sanchez."

The easiest judge in the state. Lucky me. I asked directions to the prosecutor's office, where I spoke with the young lawyer who'd be handling Rocko's hearing this afternoon. I did my best to stress the violence and instability of the guy, and recounted the visit I'd just had with him. The lawyer, who looked about six months out of school, wrote everything down and seemed to take me seriously. I had one hope here, that the guy was so eager to please that he really would make a case for locking Rocko away without bond forever.

Barring that, my best hope was to get out of the county, soon, and to change my name when I got back home.

I spent the next hour giving much the same information to

a deputy in the sheriff's office and hoping that it all came together to make a strong case against both the Rodman boys.

I came out of the building, almost surprised to see that the sun was shining and the spring flowers were blooming full force in planter boxes around the government buildings. I rubbed my arms again, to work off the chill that had settled on me and hoped my visit to the jail hadn't somehow compromised the case. My car was stuffy inside, but the heat felt good and I sat there for a few minutes, contemplating my next move.

Food. Once my fingers no longer felt like ice, I realized that it was already past midday and I was starving. Okay, technically not starving, but I knew I could put away a Big Mac without a qualm. I must have burned four thousand calories just facing down Rocko.

I ordered at the drive-through and pulled around to the lot to eat in the car. Life began to feel a little more carefree as I watched sparrows pick at fallen fries in the parking lot, fluttering away whenever a car came through, hopping back when the coast became clear again. Two young moms with little kids— clean kids without messy diapers and screaming faces—came out with Happy Meals. The seamy side of life among jail and criminals faded.

I studied the surrounding businesses as I sipped the last of my Coke. Across the street was a dry cleaning shop, a Chinese restaurant, and a place advertising that they made repairs on sewing machines, vacuum cleaners, and bicycles. The building next to the parking lot in which I sat seemed to house professional offices, including two dentists, an insurance company, and a brokerage firm. It took a minute for it to sink in that this was the same brokerage logo I'd seen on the statements from David's hidden accounts.

Before I'd clearly thought out a plan, I found myself locking the car and walking toward the place.

chapter

⊰❖ 24 ❖⊱

"**H**ow may I help you?" queried a young woman behind a counter. She appeared to be in her early twenties, maybe just out of college. I wondered how much I could really get out of her.

"My brother has several accounts with this firm," I said, making it up as I went. "He had an Albuquerque address but hasn't received his most recent statements. He's been away. He'd like me to check the current balances in the accounts."

"I'll need the full name, address, and Social Security number on the account," she said, turning to her computer.

So young, yet she'd already tripped me up.

"Mark Franklin," I told her. Somehow, I was able to recite most of the address. "I don't remember his Social at all. Can you find the information anyway?"

Her soft young look hardened. "Absolutely not. Our clients' information is strictly confidential."

"I appreciate that and I'll know I can absolutely trust you if I ever open an account here, but this is important."

The firm stare didn't waver.

"Okay, let me be honest here." I hurried on before she could make some kind of comeback to that. I whipped out my business card. "I'm with RJP Investigations in Albuquerque. The family are clients of ours. Mark has passed away and his daughter needs the information on his accounts. She inherited everything."

"We'd need her to come in, with a copy of the death certificate, and all the information I've already requested."

Now where on earth were we going to get a death certificate for Mark Franklin? This whole thing was going to get very sticky.

I thanked her, ungraciously, I'm afraid, and left. An area for Ron's expertise, perhaps.

Back in the car, I called Ron on my cell phone and posed the question to him. He thought about it for a couple of minutes and said he'd get back to me. Without any better plan in mind, I headed back toward Watson's Lake.

I'd almost made up my mind to go ahead and tell Amanda about the secret accounts. Maybe David had hinted about them at some point. I also wanted to warn her about the Rodman brothers and fill her in on my visit to the courthouse.

Afternoon shadows were beginning to cross the road as I got to the outskirts of Watson's Lake. There'd not been a cloud in the sky all day, although the weather forecast called for some rain by tomorrow. The lake gleamed like a huge turquoise stone set in the valley between the pine covered hills.

Amanda, driving Jake's vehicle, turned onto the highway Piedra Vista Road coming from her house, just as I reached the same intersection. I tooted my horn at her and she waved. I gestured and she got my meaning, pulling to the side. I stopped behind her and got out.

"I'm tracking some leads, something kind of off-topic, but thought I'd run it past you," I said.

She gave a puzzled squint and nodded.

"Have you ever heard the name Mark Franklin?"

"Mark Franklin? I don't think so."

"Other Franklins?"

"Well, that was my grandmother's maiden name. Aletha Franklin, my dad's mother. I don't know a Mark, though. Could be a cousin, I suppose. We weren't really close to any of the extended family."

"It helps, though. Puts another piece of the puzzle in place."

She gave a quizzical look but I wasn't ready to fill her in yet. "Well, I'm off to a teacher's meeting. I've told them I'm coming back to work," she said.

"I'll catch you sometime tomorrow." I waited until she drove away and I ended up following her into town. When she turned off toward the school, I went on to Michaela's office. It was a little after five and I wasn't at all sure I'd catch her, but it was worth a try.

She was climbing into her cruiser when I drove up so I did a quick stop and hopped out.

"What's up?" she asked as I approached her window.

"If Rocko Rodman was granted bail this afternoon, would we be able to find that out?"

"Why do you ask?"

I explained my visit to the jail, feeling somewhat foolish as I watched the expression on her face.

"Do you always go around asking for trouble?" she said. "Is this an intentional thing with you?"

I felt a flush of anger well up in me, but held back a sharp retort. Properly chastised, I strove for a calm voice. "He's the one who came after me, if you'll recall. He's the one who ran Amanda off the road, held up the Handy Mart, and has done who-knows-how-many other crimes. I'm just wondering at the chance of his actually being kept off the streets."

"All depends on the judge's mood today and whether the prosecutor made any kind of convincing argument."

I told her about my subsequent visit at that office.

"Anyway, I'm wondering whether I'm safe to hang around here a few more days or if I better be getting myself out of town by tonight."

Her mouth quirked into a shape that was meant to look like a smile but held a sharp edge of disgust. "Let's make a call. Easier to do it now than to come out to your motel and find your dead body sometime during the night."

I found that so reassuring. But I trotted along behind her as she unlocked the building and then her own office. She fingered through a Rolodex and dialed a number. Apparently prosecutors work later than cops because she actually got an answer. After some terse questions and a hold of at least ten minutes, she uh-huh'd a couple of times and hung up.

"Bond was set at half a million—each. It would take a miracle greater than the second coming for those guys to raise anything near enough. I think you're safe."

I told her about my Beretta and showed her my carry permit. "I'm going to have it with me," I said. "I've never drawn it on a person, and I won't unless it's life or death." The statement was at least fifty percent true.

She grumbled a little but probably decided that it was easier to let me shoot Rocko than for him to shoot me. There'd be less paperwork in the long run.

I followed her back outside and thanked her as she locked up.

"There just better not be any trouble at that motel tonight," she said. "I'm not going to be very happy if I miss my episode of CSI. And I'll be real mad if I have to get out of my nice warm bed to come down there." She started to get into the cruiser. "Oh, by the way, that tire iron? No way to narrow it to a specific vehicle, and the size would fit about two dozen different light truck or SUV models between 1987 and 2002. Not much help, I'm afraid. If the crime lab can get some kind of latent prints from it, they'll give it their best shot.

"Now you behave yourself," she said as she closed her door.

I gave her a little cross-my-heart gesture and got into my Jeep.

Back in cabin two, I kicked off my shoes, pottied, and washed my hands. Ron probably wouldn't still be at the office so I called his cell. When he answered I could hear music in the background.

"Where are you?" I asked.

"Out. I just met Victoria for a drink at Barney's."

"Ah. I was hoping to catch you at the office, but if I give you some information could you check it out first thing tomorrow?"

"Sure. Go." I heard a faint shuffling as he pulled out a pen and paper.

"I found out that Franklin was David's mother's maiden name. I'm wondering if we could fake our way into his brokerage accounts with that information. The copies of the fake ID's and Social Security numbers are in the file I set up for him, in the bottom drawer of my desk."

"And what am I looking for once I'm into the accounts?" he asked.

"I'd like to know what the current balances are now, for one thing. They've probably grown since the last statement we saw. Also, what would it take to move money out of those accounts and get it to Amanda?"

"You don't think you're getting into huge IRS shit by doing that?"

"I didn't say we'd actually move any money. I just want to know what's possible. If the feds have put some kind of freeze on the money, I'd like to know that. Amanda should get that money, eventually, but she could run into all kinds of problems if the money gets into the court system. Lawyers shouldn't end up with it, she should. There've also been hints of problems between her and Jake and I want to be sure she has a say over where the cash eventually ends up."

"Will do." He seemed antsy about getting back to Victoria so we hung up.

I flopped back on the bed and dozed. When I regained consciousness, it was dark outside and the only light filtering into the room came from the vapor light on the common. The layout of this cabin was opposite from the one I'd had before and I felt a little disoriented as I sat up. Although it was early for bedtime, I didn't much want to go out for food and aside from making a quick call to Drake I really didn't want to talk to anyone else tonight. I pulled all the drapes tightly closed, brushed my teeth, and checked the pistol. With it under the second pillow, I relaxed and fell back to sleep within minutes.

The penalty for going to sleep by eight PM is that you wake up eight hours later. And there's not much to do in a town this size at four in the morning. I brewed a cup of tea and read my book until daylight, then took a walk around the Horseshoe compound and extended it until I'd covered a good stretch of Main Street in the process. About the time I was considering popping into Jo's for coffee, I remembered that I'd left the Beretta under my pillow. It would not be a good thing if the maid came across it. I increased my speed to a slow jog and saw no sign of her.

With the Do Not Disturb sign out, I showered and tidied things up, including putting the gun into my purse. It didn't do much good to have a carry permit if I didn't actually carry the thing.

At Jo's, I pondered my next move. It felt like things were happening, just not to me. The crime lab was doing its best with the tire iron and David's car; Ron would get something going on the brokerage accounts today; with luck, Rocko would be in jail until his trial and maybe there'd be a backlog that would delay him until October or November. I might get lucky enough to piece together enough clues to pin David's murder on him in the meantime. Or not.

I decided I owed it to Amanda to give her a bit of a heads-up on the secret stash of money that David had hidden away. I wasn't sure if it was a good idea to mention numbers yet; I'd just play that by ear. I finished my omelet and coffee and headed toward the Zellingers.

No car in the driveway when I arrived. But that could mean anything. One of them could be here, or they could be out together.

I rang the bell and listened for sounds from inside the house. No answer but I thought I heard voices, something like a radio or TV set. I pressed my ear to the door but it didn't make a difference. The knob turned easily in my hand. It felt weird going into the house, even though I called out to see who might respond. Nothing.

A radio on the kitchen counter was tuned to a talk station, accounting for the voices, but it seemed strange that they'd both leave with it turned on and the front door unlocked. I walked out the back and hello'd around the back yard for a minute. Lights were on in the lab, so that probably explained it. I followed the brick walk, entered the airlock, and switched my shoes for paper booties, as per protocol.

"Jake?" I called out.

The main room seemed empty as I glanced around. He must be in the clean room. I called his name again, but something caught my eye. A file drawer stood partly open and one folder was cocked slightly out of kilter with the rest of them. Files tend to be my specialty and I couldn't resist.

The tab on the folder said Patent Info. I tiptoed to it, as much as one can in paper booties that tend to swish against the floor, and eased the file out of its slot. With one finger to mark the place I opened the folder and glanced over the top sheet. Forms for a patent application, blank ones, seemed to be all that was in the folder. I stuck it back in place. Another, thicker, folder held completed forms and a sheaf of pages that looked like blueprints. I didn't take the time to look at many of them; I wouldn't have understood them anyway. An unmarked folder, seemingly empty, had come out with this one and when I started to put the thick file back the skinny one slid to the floor.

Two computer disks and a newspaper clipping slipped partway out and I dashed to retrieve it. As I picked up the article, I couldn't resist a peek. I froze when I saw the headline: "Fire Takes Life of Sacramento Woman."

I'd seen this article, the one describing Samantha Simmons's death. My fingers went numb. What—

A sound from the other room jolted me back to the present. I jammed the article into the file and the file into the drawer. The computer disks, cupped in the palm of my hand, dropped quietly into my jacket pocket.

"Charlie?" Jake stepped from the clean room, unzipping a white jumpsuit. "What are you doing?"

I wanted so badly to look down at the file drawer, to be sure it had closed completely, but didn't dare.

"I, uh, came out to talk to Amanda but she wasn't in the house."

"Well, she's not out here." His dark eyes became sharp.

"Yeah, I just figured that out. It's just that the front door was unlocked, and I heard these voices. Turned out to be the radio." I knew I was talking way too fast and explaining way too much. I forced myself to move at a normal pace as I walked back to the airlock. "I'll give her a call later and figure out a better time."

"Shall I tell her you stopped by?" He stood less than two feet away now, staring intently at me. I tried to keep his eyes engaged so he wouldn't look back at the file drawer and figure out that I'd been snooping.

"Sure, that'd be fine. What time do you expect her back?" I pulled off the paper booties and forced myself to sit down and tie the laces on my sneakers, rather than racing out the door in my socks.

"I don't know. I'll have her call you." His voice sounded distracted, like he wanted to get back to something.

"Thanks. I'll just—" I waved toward the door.

I don't know how fast I got out of there but I sure didn't linger. I went around the side of the house, rather than going back inside, and jammed the Jeep into gear almost the minute it started. I ventured a glance over my shoulder and saw Jake round the corner of the house. In his hand, a manila folder. He started running toward me, stumbling on the uneven terrain. I gunned the Jeep.

I skidded on a curve in the gravel road and forced myself to concentrate on my driving. I'd be in big trouble if I went over

chapter

⊰**25**⊱

an embankment now.

Pieces tried to click into place as I steered carefully on the winding curves. By the time I got to the highway I was shaking so badly I pulled to the side. My head pounded with the implications. Amanda had known nothing about the fire that killed her mother, nothing about the explosion. But Jake did. I searched for an innocent explanation. Maybe David had kept the clipping for years, and wanting to protect his daughter from the knowledge, had hidden it in the unmarked file in a place she'd be unlikely to ever look. But that didn't quite ring true.

Down in my denim pocket the computer disks clacked together. I reached down and touched them. What secrets did they contain? I had no doubt Jake had hidden them away for a reason, and it couldn't be mere coincidence that they'd been in the folder with the article about the fire. There's no way I could let this go unheeded.

Sending them to Albuquerque and waiting for Ron to take a look would be out of the question. This whole thing was about to come to a head. I racked my brain for an answer. The library. They usually had public computers. I wondered whether Watson's Lake's small facility, which I'd noticed on my walk with Rusty one day, could accommodate me.

I jammed the disks deeper into my pocket and put the Jeep in gear again. As I made the left turn onto the highway I gave one more look backward but there was still no sign of Jake.

Entering the town limits, I cruised slowly, forcing myself to calm down, trying to remember on which side street I'd seen the library. I was getting impatient with myself for not spotting it, and finally pulled off Main Street at Cowboy Drive and took a left on Quarter Horse Road. Two blocks later, on a narrow lane with no street sign, I saw it. The small building matched the overall rustic style of everything else in town, and it was only the undersized sign with its burnt-wood lettering that told what the building housed. I pulled into the three-slot parking area where someone had valiantly planted an attractive garden of wildflowers at the edges. One other car sat in the lot, the librarian I assumed.

I tugged at the warped wooden door, which didn't want to yield, and felt my irritation rise. By the time I burst into the room, the noises from the squeaky door caused all heads to turn my way. A gentle-looking woman behind the desk sent a quizzical look toward me and two others—a man and a teenage girl—gave me quick glances and turned back to their computer screens. At least the presence of the computers answered my first question. The fact that there were only two machines and both were occupied drove my frustration up a notch.

"Help you?" The librarian asked.

"I was hoping to use a computer." It came out as a faint question at the end.

"There's a thirty minute limit," she said. "Someone should be done soon."

I sent her a tight smile and nodded before shuffling toward the stacks to waste a little time. Wasting time isn't something I do well and I must admit that I cleared my throat a few times and probably sighed deeply at least once. Finally, the man gathered his papers, tamped them together and got up. He gave me an apologetic look and that made me feel bad about being such a whiner. But not bad enough not to rush to the vacant chair.

I took the disks from my pocket and stared at them for a minute. They were unlabeled, as I well knew, and staring at the plastic casings wasn't giving me any additional hints about their contents. They could be documents, spreadsheets, or photos for all I knew. I chose one and inserted it into the proper drive.

A couple of clicks showed me the contents of the disk, two items which appeared to be rather short text documents. When I clicked on the first one the light blinked and the drive chattered for a few seconds then a message on the screen suggested that I use the system's default word processor to open it. I agreed with that and let the first document open.

It was a letter addressed to a Mr. Robert Rabini of MedSciences, Inc. The wording was pretty general, things along the lines of "our recent conversation" and "enclosed are the documents we discussed." A quick roll to the bottom of the page indicated that the letter was signed by David Simmons. Okay.

I read it again but didn't get much the second time either.

"Is there a printer connected to this computer?" I asked over my shoulder.

The librarian pointed to a small inkjet sitting next to the machine where the teen girl sat. Apparently both computers shared it. I printed the letter, retrieved it quickly, and opened the other. It appeared to be very similar in tone, but I printed it anyway.

The second disk proved more revealing. It contained two long documents, one text, one spreadsheet. Luckily, the computer provided me a way to open that one as well.

Detailed projections for sales over a five year period laid themselves out before me. The numbers were impressive and I glanced around with a sudden guilty feeling that I was exposing secret information to the world. The teen girl had picked up her books and was keeping the librarian occupied at the desk. I breathed relief and quickly printed the sheets. They filled ten pages, each of which I grabbed off the printer as soon as it came out.

The second document looked like a prospectus detailing Jake's research on the YA-30. It gave facts and figures and made references to the spreadsheet with the backup numbers. Again, rather than leaving the document on screen for just anyone to look at, I printed it. With one eye on the others in the room, I gathered everything neatly and retrieved my disks. By the time I reached the librarian's desk the other girl had gone and I asked how much I owed for the copies. Three dollars later I walked out to the car.

In the privacy of my own vehicle, I paged through the sheets. David had apparently sent the detailed prospectus and financial spreadsheets to this Rabini at MedSciences roughly six months before he disappeared. If memory served, I thought it was about two months after this letter that he'd banked ten million. Millions of dollars that he hadn't shared with Jake. Millions of reasons for his son-in-law to be angry enough to kill him.

I pressed my forehead against the steering wheel and breathed in and out slowly. Twice.

It was time for law enforcement to take over.

I cruised the streets until I spotted Michaela coming out of the post office. I whipped in beside her patrol SUV, and jammed my Jeep in Park at the same time I jumped out of it.

"Charlie, what?" she said, nearly dropping the stack of envelopes she'd carried out with her.

"I think I've figured out the arson. Jake Zellinger did it. He knew about David's first wife dying in a fire. It's something even Amanda didn't know about. But he's got the clipping. He knew and he set David up."

"Whoa, wait a second. What first wife?"

I'd forgotten that she probably knew nothing of this, so I quickly filled in a few of the details. "I assumed you knew," I said. "Continental Union did. That was part of the reason they assumed David set this fire. Same m.o., gas leak and boom."

She made that irritated-looking little grimace with her mouth, and I imagined the thoughts running through her head. Small town cops are never kept in the loop. Should have been her case. And on, and on.

"You've got to bring Jake in, question him," I said, bouncing on the balls of my feet like a kid desperate for the bathroom.

"And what makes you so sure he did this?"

"Money. Follow the money. It makes sense that he'd already used up the money David got from the mortgage, so he decided to go after the life insurance. If he could catch David in the house . . ." I felt my eyes go wide. "But he didn't catch David in the house, did he? He waited until David drove away . . ."

"So are you saying he also killed David?"

I hadn't been saying that at all, but suddenly it made sense. Jake's reaction when the car was found, the way his face went white. His satisfaction when Amanda got the full inheritance, his newfound solicitude toward her on the day of the funeral.

Michaela and I traded stares as it hit both of us.

"Shit fire!" she cursed as she ran for her cruiser. She tossed the stack of mail on the passenger seat and picked up her radio. "He's at their house right now?" she shouted toward me. When I nodded, she began barking orders into the microphone.

"My damn deputy's in the dentist's chair over in Segundo right now. And I can't get backup for at least another forty-five minutes from County."

I paced near the rear end of her car. "He doesn't have a vehicle," I offered. "At least it wasn't there when I arrived. Amanda was going back to work today, so she probably has it."

Michaela lowered the mike. "That's some relief," she said. "But I don't dare go up there alone."

She saw the hopeful look on my face.

"Oh, no you don't," she said. "My ass would be grass if I let a civilian go in with me."

"Not even an armed one? Not even if I just stayed in the background?"

"And then what good would you be? Just forget it. We're going to wait for backup then I'll go up there and calmly interview him. The questioning will take place right in my office."

I fidgeted, but couldn't say much.

She started to get in the cruiser.

"Can I at least wait at your office until I know you have him in custody?" I know I sounded like I was begging. "He'll know I'm behind this. I don't want to sit alone in a motel room."

I saw the slightest hint of surrender.

"You can sit in the corner, and only if you stay quiet."

Like an obedient puppy I got into my car and followed her to the village hall.

chapter

⊰ 26 ⊱

The plan sounded like a good one. Two state police officers would be here within the hour and they would accompany Michaela to the Zellinger place to bring Jake in for questioning. With that much armed muscle he wouldn't resist and he'd shed some light on both of the open cases. The plan sounded like a good one until, fifteen minutes after we'd settled into Michaela's office to wait, two calls came in.

The first came from one CJ Dettweiler, who lived two houses away from Amanda and Jake. He'd just walked out of his house in time to see Jake Zellinger driving one of his ATVs away, roaring off in a cloud of dust like he owned the thing. He'd shouted at Jake, "What the hell?"—a direct quote—but his young neighbor didn't stop. CJ said he'd have loaned Jake the machine if he'd just asked politely, but now he was mad, by god, and wanted to press charges. He'd given it a lot of thought, ten whole minutes, and yes, ma'am, he wanted to press charges.

The second call came from the principal at Amanda's school.

They had a hostage situation.

Details were sketchy but a young man with wild eyes came into Mrs. Zellinger's class, screaming foul language and grabbing the teacher.

I heard all this over the police radio on Michaela's desk, as the dispatcher relayed details from the 911 central number in Segundo.

Michaela had just finished assuring CJ Dettweiler that she was sure his ATV would be returned, while she was shooting an 'oh shit' look over at me. Now she had bigger matters to worry about. The dispatcher patched the call directly through.

I had to admire her composure as she told the school principal—I think I heard her call him Jeff—to calm down. She asked whether they'd locked down the school and he assured her they had.

"How many students are still in the classroom?" Her hand shook as she wrote down his answer. At least fifteen. They couldn't be sure. And the teacher.

"We'll be right there," she assured him. She looked at me. "Jake knows you. And you're close to Amanda. I want you to come, but—you'll stay back at all times. Is that clear?"

"Yes, ma'am." I couldn't recall the last time I'd uttered that phrase, but it was the only appropriate response right now.

I rode over to the school in the cruiser with Michaela. Her deputy had been notified to "get your ass back here, cavity or no." And we knew the state police were on the way. Now a hostage negotiator was also being flown in from Albuquerque, but that would take at least an hour. For now, all she could do was to keep the situation from becoming explosive.

The parking lot looked like a parade ground, minus the floats and bands and festivity. Groups of students stood in clusters with a teacher hovering over each, like mother hens counting their chicks. A man in a short-sleeved dress shirt, white with faint gray stripes, and a blue tie with a dot of catsup near the tip, greeted Michaela's car the minute we rolled to a stop.

"We've evacuated all the classrooms but the one," he said breathlessly. "The teachers are taking count now to see who's missing. My secretary is watching over the ones from Amanda's class, the few who got out."

"So some of them did?" Michaela asked.

"At least ten. A few of them were quick thinking enough to run when they first spotted the knife."

"Is that his only weapon?" she asked.

"As far as we know. It's all the kids have mentioned. They're over there." He pointed to a tall, blonde woman in a flowered dress and white cardigan. "Mrs. Whiteside is my secretary."

Michaela walked toward her and I trailed along, obediently quiet. The thought crossed my mind that I was probably in violation of at least twenty state and federal statutes by having the Beretta with me on school property, but I wasn't going to let it or my purse out of my sight.

"Mrs. Whiteside? Michaela Fritz." For some reason the introduction came as a surprise to me. I guess I assumed that everyone in a town this size knew absolutely everyone else.

Michaela nodded Mrs. Whiteside off a few feet away from the children. "Do we have a roll call done yet?"

"Mrs. Zellinger has twenty students in her class. Ten of them got out. I'll keep them under my care until we know what to do next."

Like magic, or as if tribal drums were rumbling an inaudible tone, word had gotten out and anxious parents in cars began to arrive. As each teacher accounted for his or her pupils, they were allowed to leave with their parents.

"No sense in keeping anyone in the vicinity who doesn't have to be here," Michaela said.

"Mrs. Zellinger's class is in the east wing," Jeff said. "She apparently has a cell phone and we've had one demand call already. During that call we ascertained that the subject and hostages are still inside the one room."

Interesting how everyone adopts television cop talk when something like this comes up.

Michaela didn't seem to notice. Her eyes darted in all directions, watching the parking lot begin to empty, eager parents clutching their kids tightly when they learned their own were all right. I noticed that she kept scanning the horizon, hoping for that helicopter with the hostage negotiator.

As soon as the deputy arrived she put him to work parking a barrier of vehicles and stringing yellow tape a safe distance from the building so police could watch the scene while they tried to talk Jake out of the building.

I thought of Amanda inside, a knife to her throat, probably, her students scared to death. If my seeing the news article set Jake off to the this extent—and I knew now with sickening certainty that I hadn't hidden the folder well enough—then the man was crazy. Who knew to what extent? He'd implanted himself with the youth formula. Was this thirty-something man now the equivalent of a hot-headed teenager? Had it affected his judgment and reasoning abilities? Or was he simply desperate to get away, to avoid facing the consequences after setting up the explosive fire and killing two people?

I stuck by Michaela's side as she took a position behind one of the parked cruisers. She'd told me to stay at the back, but she didn't object when I hunkered down beside her.

The radio at her belt crackled and she responded into the mike on her shoulder.

"I have a call from Jake Zellinger, from inside the school," said the dispatcher. "Shall I patch it through?"

Michaela gave an affirmative and the radio crackled once more. "Jake?" she said.

"I'll let the kids go if you let me and Amanda out of here, unhurt, and if you don't come after me."

The sheriff closed her eyes for a moment, as if in prayer. "Let the kids out now, Jake, and we can certainly talk about the rest of it. I think we can work something out."

"I'm not going to prison for this," Jake shouted. "He deserved it. Double-crosser!"

Michaela looked worried. "Calm down, Jake. Let's talk about it."

His voice became shrill. "He got what he deserved! I should have had that money!"

The sheriff fumbled for words. "What's he talking about?" she whispered to me.

"I think I know. Want me to try?"

She handed me the mike.

"Jake, it's Charlie." I forced my voice to stay low and calm. "I'm out here with the sheriff. Is Amanda okay?"

I heard a whimper in the background.

"Jake, could I speak to Amanda for a second?" As if I were calling their house and just wanted a little girl chat. I hoped changing the subject would get his mind off the money momentarily.

"Charlie?" Her voice sounded quavery and small.

"Amanda, how are the kids? Are there ten of them with you?"

A short pause. "Yes, we're doing all right."

"Can you persuade him to let the kids out?"

"I've tried that."

Jake's voice came back as he yanked the phone away from her. "Enough, Charlie. The kids are fine, Amanda's fine. I want the money and I want Amanda and myself out of here."

"We found the money, Jake. We've got it for you."

"You did?" He perked up. "No, you didn't. You're making that up so I'll come out."

"No, Jake. It's true. The money's in some accounts in Albuquerque. We found out about them and I was going to ask you about them."

I glanced at Michaela and she looked hopeful. She gave me a wrist-rolling motion, saying, go on, go on.

"David double crossed me," Jake said, more reasonably this time. "He sold the patent without my knowledge. I found the paperwork, but not the money. I just wanted my share. I spent my life inventing the YA-30. It wasn't his to sell. I just wanted my share." His voice had become shaky and I was afraid of sending him over the edge again.

"Jake, it's okay. Come out, we'll get everything straight. You'll get your money."

Off in the distance the distinct sound of a helicopter began to work into my consciousness. I scanned the horizon and saw its tiny profile, five or six miles away. The sound grew louder and the dot bigger with each passing second.

"Charlie?" Jake's voice edged upward again. "What's that sound? Who's coming?"

"It's a negotiator from Albuquerque. They sent for someone to talk to you."

"I'm talking to you. That's no negotiator. They're sending somebody to drop tear gas on me or something. They're gonna bomb the building!"

Shit, how could this have gone so wrong? The helicopter was within a mile now, circling to get the lay of the land.

"No, Jake, they're not doing anything like that."

In the background, I heard Amanda shriek. Several tiny voices screamed.

"Jake, Jake, listen to me. You don't want to hurt anybody in there. That's not smart. You're a smart guy, Jake. You want to get the money, don't you?" I rattled on, saying anything I could think of. "Jake, the guy in the helicopter, he's bringing the money."

"That's a lie, Charlie. There's no way he had time to get it and bring it. You're lying, you bitch!"

Oh, god, what have I done? I silently handed the mike back to Michaela.

"Jake," she said in her most grandmotherly voice.

The pilot spotted our barricade and brought the ship down in a vacant field behind us. As the rotor wound down, a man in Kevlar gear stepped out. Ducking low, he ran toward us. The aircraft took off again, apparently to find a spot out of the range of gunfire, if it should come to that. When I could hear again, I noticed Michaela talking.

"Jake, Jake?" she said into the mike. She turned to the negotiator, who tersely introduced himself as Butch. "He's not answering."

He raised a bullhorn and aimed it toward the building. "Jake, my name is Butch. I'm here to help everyone get out of there safely."

Michaela's microphone spewed forth some static. Amanda's voice came through. "He's gone," she said, tiredly. "He took off out back."

"What?" Michaela said.

"He got out the back of the building while it was so noisy. The kids and I are okay."

"Stay in there, lock the room until we know it's safe."

The back of the building. I raised my head to get a look and figure out what she was talking about. The back of the building led to an open playground and I didn't see anyone out there. But he could have crept around the side, toward the street. And toward the parking lot full of cars, and toward the people who were still milling around out there.

At that moment I heard a scream from the parking area. I bumped Michaela's arm and pointed.

A car, which had been casually driving toward the exit, now picked up speed and careened onto the street, narrowly missing a little girl and her mother. As the tires hit pavement, it squealed. Horns blared as it apparently came to the intersection with Main Street. I couldn't tell; I was running toward the hub of excitement in the parking lot.

Jeff, the principal stood there, gripping a hysterical woman by the shoulders.

"What happened?" I asked, my breath coming out in giant huffs.

"My car! He grabbed— Aaron's in there! The backseat!"

Jeff looked around helplessly.

Michaela and Butch had seen me take off and they arrived and began drilling questions at the woman. She collapsed in sobs and Jeff walked her to an open car door where she could sit down.

"Jake stole a car and there's a little boy in the back seat," I said, working to keep my voice steady.

"You handle the ground chase, we'll keep him in sight," Butch told Michaela. He took off at a dead run toward the helicopter. He barked orders into a handheld radio and I could hear the pilot bring up the rotor speed.

For the first time, I noticed two State Police vehicles near the school gates. They must have just arrived. I pointed them out to Michaela and she gratefully ran toward them.

I found myself standing alone in a tiny island of calm while pandemonium went on around me. Then I spotted Amanda, a diminutive mama bird surrounded by her brood, coming out of the building. A trickle of blood ran from her jawline and disappeared inside the collar of her sweater.

Tears welled in my eyes as I watched her herd the little ones to the sidewalk. An outcry erupted as moms whose kids had been in the midst of the horror rushed to pair up with them. Amanda made sure each child was safe before she tried to take in the rest of the scene. When she spotted me her face began to quiver. I walked over and put my arms around her and let her lean into me.

The helicopter rose, kicking up a dust cloud, and making a smooth pedal turn to locate the speeding car. They headed east, roaring over the school yard. I noticed that both state patrol cars had headed out in the same direction, where Main Street would lead him out of town, or to the numerous side roads which climbed into the mountains. I had no idea at this point which way Jake would go, and only hoped he would feel some measure of care for the little boy in the backseat.

Michaela had moved her cruiser to the school gate, where she parked to form a barricade and was telling everyone to calm down and stay put. They were safer inside the gates than out on the road where anything could happen. I steered Amanda to a grassy spot in front of the building and offered a clean tissue, which did little to remove the blood trail. It had pretty well dried in place.

"What's going to happen?" she asked. I knew her concern was more for the child in the car than for her husband.

chapter

⋊27⋉

Collectively, we the crowd watched the helicopter, our only point of reference by now, as the pilot followed a straight course along the highway, toward the lake. I wondered, in one of those fleeting thoughts that zips through your mind, whether Jake might just drive off the boat ramp, burying the car as he'd done with David's.

But the aircraft kept circling, working its way farther south as Jake apparently went off on side roads. After twenty minutes or so, it hovered over one place. The chase was over.

I left Amanda sitting on the grass, where other teachers, kids, and parents who hadn't gotten off the school grounds earlier, formed a little cluster. Amanda actually got them to playing word games, taking their minds off the drama on the other side of the valley.

Jeff kept Aaron's mother isolated, an incoherent mass of fear and uncertainty. I wanted to offer consolation of some kind, but had no clue what I might say that could make the situation any better. I walked over to Michaela who stood at the open door of her cruiser, one foot on the running board, microphone at her mouth.

"They've stopped the vehicle," she said when the voice at the other end paused. "Jake's in custody."

"What about the little boy? His mother is frantic."

· She held up a hand and listened to the fuzzy transmission. "He's okay. Shaky and crying, but unhurt."

"Shall I?" I nodded toward the mom.

"Please."

I walked back to Jeff and gave him a thumbs up. When the woman saw this she collapsed again in fresh weeping.

"I'm sure they'll bring him down very soon," I told her.

She grinned broadly with her red, watery face. Two other women, who'd been huddled nearby, saw this and the word soon spread. Relief spread like a visible blanket over the crowd.

"You seem to know things about this situation that the rest of us don't," Michaela said to me when I walked back to her vehicle. "What money?"

I hedged. "I made up a lot of that," I said. "Just anything to make Jake think he should give up."

"You got information out of him, though. Motive for the murder."

I tried to shrug it off but she went on.

"I want you to be there when we question him. One of the state guys is driving Aaron back here to his mom, and the other is transporting Jake to Segundo. You and I will follow in my car." It wasn't a question or a request. I was going.

* * *

The interrogation room at the State Police building in Segundo was a lot like those I imagined from Law and Order, except a lot smaller. On TV there's always a long table in a big room, suspect on one side, good cop and bad cop on the other. Here, we had an eight-by-eight room with seven people jammed into it: Jake (with a goose-egg bump on his forehead, a fat lip, and a swath of blood from a cut near his eyebrow— the police said he'd been stopped by a forty-foot pine tree); two homicide detectives, Michaela, the original arson investigator, and a guy Continental Union had rushed in on a moment's notice. Oh, and me.

The lead interrogator started with the stuff we knew: Jake had already admitted that David had sold their patent without telling him. That accounted for the uneasy looks I'd picked up the day those businessmen asked him about the patent paperwork. Of course, I hadn't picked up on that from the patent file; it was too full of complex-looking forms and diagrams and paperwork. Maybe David counted on Jake's focus on the research and his disinterest in paperwork to somehow keep the money angle distant. That could work for awhile, but ultimately Jake would want to know where his share had gone. David had provided Jake with all the motive he needed.

We also knew David had been murdered, how and where he'd ended up. With a little fill-in-the-blank, the interrogator managed to start Jake talking.

"I found out he'd sold the patent one day when I was at David's house," he said. "He'd gone outside for something and the phone rang. The guy started right out talking, not realizing I wasn't David, and I put it together."

Jake sat on one side of the table with the two homicide detectives facing him. The rest of us filled the nooks and corners of the room.

His fists clenched as he remembered the day. "I just saw red. I made an excuse to leave and got the hell out of there. I went home, thinking it must be a mistake. David had arranged the sale but just hadn't told me about it. I spent twelve hours a day in the lab, and he hadn't had time to tell me. But two more days went by and he never said a word. Went along like before, like everything was just the same." His face hardened. "That bastard was out to cheat me. I figured it out."

I watched as the various investigators scratched notes on pads.

"I called him one afternoon. He was supposed to leave for Denver that day but I suggested he come out to the house on the way. Earleen was in Santa Fe for the day, so she'd never know and Amanda had a teacher's meeting that night."

"So, how did you get him out to the lake?" the second homicide guy asked.

"I wasn't at the house when he got there. I called his cell

phone and told him some phony reason I had to go to the marina. Asked him to meet me there instead. He came." Jake shrugged at David's gullibility.

"And you knocked him over the head."

Jake shrugged again. His braggadocio wasn't going to extend to a full confession.

Michaela tapped one of the interrogators on the shoulder and whispered something in his ear. He looked at me and nodded. "I believe you've made a connection with the arson?"

I felt all eyes on me and my mouth went dry. Michaela gave me a nudge.

"During our own investigation, at the request of Mrs. Amanda Zellinger," I said, "we discovered an interesting bit from David Simmons's past. A previous home of his had exploded due to a gas leak. Earlier today I was in Jake Zellinger's lab and saw a copy of the same article about that. Clearly, Jake knew something about the first fire, something Amanda had not known until very recently."

The interrogator turned to Jake. "So you set it up to look like David had torched his own house."

Again, Jake gave him a cool stare but didn't admit to the crime.

"You knew there was hardly a chance David's body would be found, that people would assume he set the gas leak himself and went into hiding." The man gave Jake a cold stare. "You gave yourself a good long time to search for the money in the meantime."

Questions began flying from all corners of the room, and the more they talked the cooler Jake became. The collected bodies began to generate more heat that I could handle, plus I had the irresistible urge to whip out the rubber hoses and beat the truth out of the hard little man who sat before us. I excused myself to Michaela and edged out the door.

⊰28⊱

B y the time I got back to my cabin—after waiting for Michaela to finish tedious hours of questions, and the long drive back to Watson's Lake—I wanted nothing more to do with humankind. I decided to dine on a cup of tea and a package of peanut butter crackers that I'd purchased in desperation from a vending machine at the police station.

No such luck. Amanda was waiting on my porch, sitting in the chair and rocking with a zombie-like rhythm.

"I couldn't face going home," she said as I climbed the porch steps. "I hope you don't mind."

What could I say? My mother raised me with better manners than that.

"Are you hungry?" I asked.

She shook her head slowly.

"Where have you been all this time?" I asked.

A tiny smile crossed her face. "In my classroom. Thinking. Straightening the desks and re-hanging the art projects so it'll seem normal tomorrow. Thinking."

"Will you be up to going back tomorrow?"

"How can I not? The kids went through the same trauma I did. I need to be there for them. And I can't sit around the house. It's going to be weird, going back there."

I nodded an acknowledgement and unlocked the door. I dropped my purse on the bed. "You want to use the bathroom or anything?"

She caught my meaning and reached up to touch the dried blood on her neck. "I guess I—yeah, I better."

My stomach was beginning to speak to me and I debated how far I could stretch the peanut butter crackers between two people. I still didn't want to go out and sit in a brightly lit place.

"Is there anyplace in this town we could call and have a pizza delivered?" I called out to Amanda through the closed bathroom door.

She opened the door, holding a washcloth to her neck. "Afraid not. The Owl makes a pretty decent veggie supreme, though. We could call it in and bring it back here." I saw a faint glimmer of something positive in her face.

"I'll do it." I found the number and was told it would be ready in twenty minutes. The time went slowly, both of us avoiding the subject foremost on our minds. I kept looking at my watch.

"Charlie?" Amanda said. The twenty minutes were up and I had one hand on the doorknob. "He did it, didn't he?"

I looked across the room at her upturned face. She seemed younger, vulnerable.

"He admitted enough that the state's got a pretty strong case, but he wouldn't actually confess." I hedged. "I think he did it, yes."

Ten minutes later, when I got back with the pizza, she'd clearly been crying but she composed herself and brightened at the sight of the food. The Owl wasn't technically supposed to sell packaged liquor but when the owner found out it was for Amanda he gave me a nice bottle of burgundy. We poured it into the cabin's plastic cups and raised them.

"To a better life from this day on," Amanda said.

Very content with my own life, I nonetheless wished her toast would come true for her.

After two slices each, we seemed to regain some energy. "I need to know about it," she said. "And I'd rather hear it now, from you, than through the newspaper accounts and gossip that are going to start up. Tell me. Please."

I recounted Jake's answers to the interrogators, the fact that he'd lured David to the lake, the way he'd set the gas leak to look similar to the other one thirty years earlier, in hopes of making it look like David had done it.

"There's some money, Amanda. I don't know how much it will turn out to be. There will probably be a lot of taxes owed."

"I gathered that, from Jake's end of the conversation there in the school. Dad sold the patent, didn't he?"

"Yes, apparently so."

"And he lied to Jake and that's what set him off."

"That's what he says."

She gazed at an unseen point in the middle of the room, an unfocused stare. "I can almost believe Jake's part in all this. Ever since he tried that youth formula on himself he's become more impetuous, less able to control these spontaneous urges, very hot-headed. I've watched him change drastically from the earnest student I met ten years ago." She took another sip of her wine. "But my dad? The lies and deceit. I never saw that in him. I guess it's been there for awhile, but I'm having a hard time with it."

Tears overflowed and ran down both cheeks. She sat there quietly, letting them fall in large dots on her lap. I leaned back in my chair and left the silence alone.

"I'm going to have to talk to Jake," she finally said. "I have some things to say, and I'm not going to be at his trial. I won't be the steadfast little wife, standing by him no matter what. Whatever my father did to Jake, he didn't deserve to die for it." She stood up.

"Should you be alone at home tonight?" I asked.

"I won't be," she said with a little smile. "I've already booked a cabin here. My kids will just have to see me in the same clothes tomorrow."

"Good for you."

I woke early the next morning, with the smell of leftover pizza and unwashed wine glasses filling the room. I'm not one who's fond of cold pizza for breakfast so I gathered the box and glasses and carried them out to the dumpster at the back of the complex.

"Morning, Charlie," Amanda called out from the porch of cabin five.

"Hey. You sleep okay?"

"Wonderfully, actually." I had to admit that she looked better than she had in days. "I reread Dad's letter about fifteen times last night. Somewhere between the lines I think he was telling me that he knew about the problems between Jake and me. He said no matter what, I'd be taken care of. I have to believe that somehow it's all going to work out." She lifted her purse strap to her shoulder. "I'm going to put in my day at school, help the kids see that a person really can work past their problems, and then I'm driving up to Segundo to talk to Jake. I found out who's representing him, and he arranged it.

"By this weekend, I'll have divorce proceedings underway, the house listed on the market, and a new apartment lined up."

"Wow, when you move, you move. I admire that."

"Hey, no point in wallowing in misery."

I thought about that as I loaded my bag in the Jeep and checked out of the Horseshoe.

chapter

⊰ 29 ⊱

During the month that followed, I spent a couple of weekends with Drake in tiny motels in out-of-the-way towns—whatever happened to be near his firebase at the time. Rusty came along and we had long walks in the woods, comfortable talks in cozy beds, and old-fashioned burgers in dimly lit bars.

In June, temperatures hit record highs with the weather people talking about the number of consecutive triple-digit days, a rarity for Albuquerque. When the heat finally broke, the seasonal rains—which we frivolously call monsoons—came early. This was good on several fronts. Drake got to come home early, the mountains received much-needed moisture, and tempers cooled along with the weather.

We were heading into the Fourth of July weekend when I heard from Amanda. I knew I would; we'd been finalizing a folder of information for her, including the complete data we'd compiled on her father's secret brokerage accounts. I'd also asked around and gotten recommendations for a good tax attorney she should talk to.

We met for lunch at a cute downtown restaurant, where the prices tended to be right on par with the classy décor.

"You look great, Charlie," she greeted as I walked in the door.

I had to admit that she did, too. She'd put on a few pounds and the gaunt, harried look was gone. She'd had her hair restyled and the lighter, layered look complimented her face.

I tucked the folder of information along the side of my chair as we sat down, and we spent the first few minutes in pleasantries and placing our orders for salads. She waited until we'd finished eating before bringing up the big subjects.

"I talked to Jake," she said. "I think I told you I was planning to."

"How'd it go?"

"There wasn't a lot he could say. I told him I'd put his share of the proceeds from the house sale toward his defense, and the law firm representing him was glad to get it. I made it clear, though, that it was all they'd get from me. Considering that they'd planned to take the case pro bono, they seemed happy to get anything.

"Bless his heart, he told me he hadn't really loved me for years. He'd been staying with me 'out of pity' he said, because he knew I couldn't manage without him. When I posed the possibility that he'd really stayed on because he wanted to come across the money Dad had received from the sale of the patent, he actually admitted it. He thought that admission would hurt me, I guess. But I think I knew it all along. Hearing it didn't bother me a bit."

I had to marvel at her composure.

"We're divorced now—it was final two weeks ago. I changed my name back to Simmons because Zellinger is going to be making the news a little too much in coming months." She took a sip from her iced tea. "Luckily, the house sold right away. And did you hear? Earleen and Frank packed up and left. Rumor has it they went out of state and Frank plans to get back into construction."

And I'd about bet money that his past illegalities wouldn't be mentioned.

"I'm going to take Dad's life insurance money and build on his property. Something cozy and just the right size for me."

I picked up the folder. "You won't be limited on funds," I said. "You can build a showplace if you want to."

I opened the folder and watched her eyes widen when she saw the numbers. I pointed to the business card clipped to the front of the folder. "You'll want to call this man before you do anything else. He comes highly recommended."

She slowly paged through the brokerage statements. "I had no idea."

"You should know that the IRS was looking for your dad. Or, I should say, they were looking for Mark Franklin. They're going to want a chunk of this. Have a nice long talk with the attorney first. Let him handle it. Whatever's left will be yours."

"If there's even a tenth of this left over, it's huge," she said. She looked up at me with moist eyes.

"It'll be a lot more than ten percent. But I have no idea how much."

"I can't even fathom . . ."

I closed the folder, tucked it into her hands. "You will. You'll figure out something."

That was the last time I saw Amanda Simmons. I got one note from her, around Christmas. She'd included a check, although I'd not submitted a bill to her. It more than covered our expenses. She'd netted a decent seven-figure sum from the accounts and told me she'd decided to keep just a little for her eventual retirement. The rest was going to a variety of charities, providing a happy end to the old year—for everyone.

ORLAND PARK
PUBLIC LIBRARY
A Natural Connection

**14921 Ravinia Avenue
Orland Park, IL 60462**

**708-428-5100
orlandparklibrary.org**